Connecting Dots

A Gutsy Girl Book

Connecting Dots

SHARON JENNINGS

Second Story Press

Library and Archives Canada Cataloguing in Publication

Jennings, Sharon, author
Connecting dots / by Sharon Jennings.

(A gutsy girl book)
Issued in print and electronic formats.
ISBN 978-1-927583-62-3 (pbk.).—ISBN 978-1-927583-67-8 (epub)

I. Title. II. Series: Gutsy girl book

PS8569.E563C65 2015 jC813'.54 C2014-908139-1

C2014-908140-5

Edited by Kathryn Cole
Designed by Melissa Kaita
Cover by Gillian Newland

Printed and bound in Canada

Second Story Press gratefully acknowledges the support of the Ontario Arts Council and the Canada Council for the Arts for our publishing program. We acknowledge the financial support of the Government of Canada through the Canada Book Fund.

Canada Council for the Arts
Conseil des Arts du Canada

Published by
Second Story Press
20 Maud Street, Suite 401
Toronto, ON M5V 2M5
www.secondstorypress.ca

With gratitude to CANSCAIP

First Page!

Leanna Mets is the most annoying person I have ever met in my life. She is also my best friend. She is writing a book. She has said so over and over and over. It is about meeting me. About how her life changed when we met in July. She wants to be a writer when she grows up.

The really annoying part is she thinks *I* should write about *my* life. I told her I have too many other things going on. I auditioned and got into the Kids for Kids Theater Company, and we're doing a play, and I have a drama exam in the spring. And schoolwork.

Yesterday, I went to Leanna's new apartment for a sleepover. She moved there in September and now we live about an hour apart. She showed me her story so far. "You made some stuff up," I said. She called it *embellishing*.

"You take the truth, but make it a little worse or a little better. So it's stronger for your book," she said. "It keeps your reader enthralled. *Enthralled* means to charm or captivate. Even enslave. I looked it up." (That is another reason why she is so annoying – always finding words in the dictionary and boring me to death.)

"I don't have to embellish anything," I assured her. "My story is too strong exactly how it is."

Leanna looked at me hopefully. She really wants to know about my past. She knows I'm not an orphan. She asks questions, and hints, but I've spent seven years lying. Do I want to tell the truth? Can I?

On the way home, I started thinking. Maybe I *should* write something. Who knows? I am going to be an actress. Maybe I'll turn my life into a book, and the book into a movie.

And so I am sitting at *my* desk in *my* room. This is very important. I've lived in guest rooms/spare rooms/hallways for five years, and now I have my *own* bedroom at Peter and Mary's. When I got here in August, the room they gave me was white and bare. "We want you to express yourself," Mary said. I didn't believe her. We went shopping the next day, and I picked out orange and green sheets and a black bedspread and pink paint and purple cushions. She looked confused, but she said, "Cool. You're rebelling. I can dig that. Whatever you want, Cassie." I realized she meant it. I went from feeling so superior and "I'll show you" to feeling embarrassed by her kindness. And mad at myself for forgetting I wanted to start fresh this time. I put everything down and asked for help. So now my room is shades of gold and red and orange – like leaves in fall. "Like your hair," said Leanna, on her first visit. I laid out Grandma's brush set and put Leanna's rock on my desk.

Where to start? I am almost twelve years old, and some of my childhood is fuzzy. But some memories are sharply focused. I guess my mind recorded lots of things, whether I wanted it to or not.

When I was little, I had a puzzle book. "Connect the Dots," it instructed. "You'll be amazed at what will emerge!" So I drew, dot to dot, until I saw a cat or a dog or a tree.

My life is one big connect the dots. And I haven't a clue what will emerge.

Hope I'm…amazed.

Chapter One

Until I was five, I thought my grandmother was my mother. In kindergarten, I found out the truth.

A girl, her long blonde hair in ringlets, carefully curled. She looked up when I entered the schoolyard. My "mother's" hand gently shoving me forward. "Go on, now, Cassie. Play nice. Make friends."

Then "Mother" was gone – out of the schoolyard and, by end of day, out of my life.

Her hands on her hips. Turning to look at me. Lifting one hand and pointing. Saying to the other girls, "That's her. That's Cassie. My mama says she's ill. Cause *her* mama was a bad girl." She laughed and the others laughed with her like they were puppets and she pulled their strings.

They linked arms and skipped away, ringlets and pigtails and ponytails bouncing up and down, saddle shoes still so clean and white.

"Nobody wants to play with me," I said after school. "Patty told them I'm sick. She said you're bad." I remember acting the whole thing out – exactly how Patty stood, how she moved, the smugness in her voice, how they all laughed.

Grandma told me then, but my memory isn't clear. There was cocoa. I felt dread – something awful about to happen – whenever I smelled cocoa after that.

So at five years old I found out my mother was dead, and this woman I lived with was my grandmother. My mother's mother. It was my mother who was ill, not me. It was my mother who got sick and died. Patty had it wrong. My grandmother was young enough to pretend she was my mother. Something about "stopping tongues wagging" she said.

I lifted my mug to my mouth, but the taste of Fry's Cocoa – Grandma forgot to put in the sugar – got linked with the word *dead* and plugged my throat.

Often I called Grandma "mother," forgetting. But I was five and at five kids go along with what they are told. When you're a kid you can ask someone *why*? and when they say *because* you just nod as if *because* is the greatest explanation of all time.

"But why was she bad?" I asked. "Patty said she was a bad girl."

Grandma started chopping vegetables with a *whack, whack, whack!* "Little minds, Cassie. *Whack!* Just crazy talk. *Whack!* Don't listen to her or anybody. *Whack!*"

It makes sense it was the following day, this next memory of mine, for I remember marching up to Patty and telling her she was cuckoo. I remember putting my hands on my hips – imitating her – and saying, "You're cuckoo, Patty Huggins. Your mind is little, like an ant's. So there!"

And then in our corner store, seeing Patty's mother – but how did I know it was Patty's mother? Is there an incident I've forgotten? I saw her and hid behind Grandma, glad for once she was fatter than the other "mothers."

"Shirley Jovanovich. I've been meaning to speak to you. It's between you and the good Lord what you want to tell that brat, but don't you dare let her talk to my Patty like that ever again."

Grandma, arms folded across her chest. "Mary Huggins. I've been meaning to speak to you as well. How you can call yourself a decent Christian woman is beyond me. Teach that child of yours some manners."

"At least she *is* a child of mine. And not some mockery of what's right."

"I go to church every Sunday same as you, Mary. I

know what's right. I know what the Lord wants me to do for this innocent child."

"Innocent! Ha! You know as well as I do, Shirley, the sins of the fathers *and* the mothers are visited upon the children until the seventh generation. You didn't do right by your own daughter, and it wouldn't surprise me in the least if *she* (peering around my grandmother to point at me) didn't turn out the same way. I've a good mind to talk to the authorities. It is my Christian duty. You're not fit to mother another girl."

"You do that, Mary Huggins. You do that. But then I might think it is *my* Christian duty to have a word with the minister about the money missing from the missionary fund. Don't think I haven't suspected the truth of *that*, Mary Huggins."

I remember two things happening afterward. One, Grandma bought a brick of ice cream and let me have three slices – unheard of! Two, my life improved. Patty invited me to play games with the others. She even said she was sorry. "Your mother wasn't bad. I heard wrong, was all."

The others followed her lead, and kindergarten was suddenly, magically, a kaleidoscope of stories and songs and crayons and finger-paints and naps and cookies with milk.

Unfortunately, I liked playing with the boys better than the girls. Boys didn't care if my hair wasn't brushed. Boys didn't notice grass stains on my knees. Boys didn't mind if I won at boogers or could spit farthest. But then the teacher caught me kissing Brian Perna under the slide.

("Just like her mom," Patty's father snickered when he heard. Or so Patty told me the next day.)

I was marched to the principal's office. He called Grandma. I was told kissing boys was bad. Grandma didn't argue – very meek for her – and at home I was sent to my room until supper. Supper was a quiet meal. When I tried to talk, Grandma shushed me. I heard her say something about maybe biting off more than she could chew, which I didn't understand because we were having soup.

Chapter Two

I had one photograph of my mother, Rita. She is fifteen and in grade nine.

"Oh!" I remember saying. "She's so pretty!"

Grandma said "Yup," without smiling.

And I remember, too, feeling relieved. Maybe I would grow up to look like her.

"Did she have lots of friends?" I asked hopefully.

"Mmmm. She was popular. No doubt about *that*." And then she mumbled, "Too popular," thinking I didn't hear. But how could a girl be too popular? It seemed like heaven to me.

It was a black-and-white photograph, but I knew she had red hair like me. She was wearing a very tight sweater, and for years I thought there was something wrong with her body – her breasts were very sharp and pointy, not rounded and droopy like the other mothers I knew. Her hair was parted on one side and pulled back tight with a barrette from her forehead, and it fell in soft waves to her shoulders. She was leaning back on a stone garden wall, and I could see a tiny waist belted tight. She was smiling and seemed to be looking right at me.

Grandma didn't have very many photos of Rita, and the others were either blurred or taken from far away. I slipped the picture out of the yellowing plastic page of the album and hid it in my bedroom.

I was in grade two when Grandma died. That was the beginning of all the moving around and being handed off to a bunch of relatives who didn't want me. And the first aunt and uncle who took me in made sure there were no photos of Rita around. Aunt Mabel (Grandma's sister, but she said "Don't you dare call me Great Aunt or I'll smack you one. See if I don't.") found the photo album and pulled out the few of my mother. I watched her put a match to the pile and when there were only greasy ashes left, she wiped her hands – *wipe, wipe, wipe* – and said "Good riddance to bad rubbish."

Grandma musta noticed the picture was missing from the album. I swapped a couple around so the hole wasn't as obvious, but still. She was a sharp woman and nothing much got by her. After she told me my mother was dead, I did wonder why there weren't any framed pictures of her displayed proudly on dressers and the mantle. Sometimes kids just know there are things no one talks about. So I swiped the photo and didn't tell and found a hiding spot. Not under my mattress, because Grandma flipped the mattress over once a month for airing, and I was afraid she'd take it back. I put it in an envelope and taped it under my bureau.

In the summer before grade two, Grandma lost weight and her housedresses hung on her, as if she was wearing clothes that belonged to someone else. Her skin looked gray, as if the blood had been drained out. Not even a walk in fresh air brought color to her cheeks, and when she put on her face, she looked more like a doll than a real person.

And soon she stopped going for walks or doing any cooking or cleaning, and then she stopped getting out of bed except to go to the bathroom. I pretended not to hear the loud gurgle of her diarrhea. I pretended not to notice the awful smell in the bathroom after. I've never forgotten that smell. We had a huge can of Lysol, but that didn't help. I learned to light matches.

I know now it was cancer, but no one talked about cancer in those days. I only found out because once when I was playing Barbies at Karen's house I heard her mother talking to Susan's mother.

They looked over at me to see if I was listening. And I was, but I knew how to look dumb. This is how kids find out things. I heard the word *Shirley* and listened doubly hard.

Karen and I swapped dresses and changed our Barbie dolls' outfits and Karen's mother whispered, "They say it's cancer, Marie," and from the corner of my eye, I saw her nod her chin in my direction.

"No! And her always so proud," Marie said back, sounding pleased. "And all that about Anton, too."

Karen's mother added, "The hypocrisy! They say only dirty people get cancer. Not so much for Shirley to be proud of now, is there?"

So Susan's mother, Marie, whispered back, "Oh, I know, Joan! Dreadful. Should we...I mean...do you think it's quite all right that Cassie plays with our girls?"

"Oh! I hadn't thought. But surely, dear, it isn't *catching*?"

Catching! I could catch what Grandma had? This dirty thing? I might soon look so tired and not be able to eat and start moaning and have stinky poops and cry at night? I jumped up, scattering the dollhouse furniture. "I have to go."

Karen's mother said, "Well, my goodness, Cassie! Be a lady and go without announcing your business. You know where the bathroom is."

"I mean, I have to go home." And I remember running out of that house and down the street to Grandma, as if I was in a race.

"What is cancer?" I demanded.

"Why, Cassie! What made you – "

"They said it's dirty and you're dirty and I might catch it."

She tried to push herself up from her pillows, knocking her teacup from its saucer. Pain spread over her face and she lay back down. "Who said?"

So I explained and I could see she was angry and sad, and she closed her eyes and shook her head, and I heard her whisper, "Give me strength."

"I don't like those mothers," I said. "They think they're so…so swish. But they're not. Karen said her mom takes lots of dresses from the rummage sale and remakes them. Karen said her father doesn't give her mother a big enough dress allowance and so she pretends she buys her clothes all the way downtown in Eaton's. Karen says…" I trailed off as a memory came into focus. "Couldn't you scare Karen's mom with that? Like you did with Patty's mom and the missionary fund? That sure shut her up, didn't it?"

Grandma's mouth twitched upwards, as if she was trying to smile but couldn't remember how. "You are a scallywag, aren't you?" She sighed and said, "But no, Cassie, I'm not going to threaten anybody. Don't have the energy for it."

Then she explained about cancer. Something grows on the inside of you. She said she was doing what she could to stay strong and get well.

And when I heard the moaning at night, I put my pillow over my head and told myself there was nothing to worry about.

Chapter Three

Bringing Grandma buttered toast and tea and telling her she had to eat. Making Campbell's tomato soup and holding a spoon to Grandma's mouth. Wiping the dribble from her chin. Holding the hot water bottle to the spot on her back that she rubbed until her skin was raw. Feeling very much a grown-up lady taking care of the invalid. She stopped going out of the house and I stopped going to school. A neighbor noticed, and my teacher came to call. Grandma's sister, Aunt Mabel, arrived and took Grandma to the hospital, and I was not allowed to visit.

Mabel said, "Children are not permitted in a hospital and that's that."

Mabel made me go to school every day and gave me

sandwiches made with a slice of corned beef all congealed with fat from a tin. "Grandma never gives me corned beef sandwiches. I hate corned beef. I like peanut butter and grape jelly."

"You'll eat what you're given, Cass Jovanovich, and be grateful for it. There are starving children in Africa, and I'll thank you to remember your blessings."

At some point many relatives showed up. At least they said they were relatives, but I hadn't met them before. Some of them stayed in the house, and I could hear them talking, but when I tried to listen, someone said "Little jugs have big ears."

They meant me, and afterwards they were careful not to talk when I was around, and I was always being shooed out to play. I asked about Grandma, but someone else said "Children should be seen and not heard."

I finally figured out who these strangers were. Great Aunt Mabel and Great Aunt Hazel were Grandma's sisters. They didn't like Grandma. Hazel brought her daughter, Lana (with husband Dick), but Mabel's daughter, Liz, was away somewhere. One day, the great uncles, Fred and Ernie, arrived.

I couldn't figure out how these people worked as relations. Hazel and Mabel looked so much older than Grandma. How could they be sisters? One day, I said so.

"That's the Irish for you," a man said. "Breeding away year after year, like barn animals."

Grandma took me to the Royal Winter Fair once, so I knew about barn animals, but what he said didn't make sense.

"You know. They could have adult kids and they're still doing it." Then he winked. I turned away. There was something smarmy about him. *Smarmy* – one of Grandma's words.

Hazel is the oldest of the three sisters and told me plainly – "I'm telling you plainly, Cass" – she didn't approve of her sister raising me. "Shirley should have put you up for adoption straightaway." She pounded her fist in her other hand. "Straight-*pound*-a-*pound*-way-*pound*. Would have saved us all a lot of shame and now a lot of trouble."

Shame and trouble. She meant me.

I didn't understand the word *adoption*. But, as usual, kids at school were ready to share their vast knowledge.

"It means you're not wanted by your real parents," Karen said, "so they get rid of you. Like too many kittens."

"Another family takes you, and pretends you're theirs," Susan added. "But you're not."

"And I heard you get hand-me-down clothes and the *real* kids get better." Alice.

"And the *real* kids don't like you." Debbie.

"And fewer presents on your birthday." Karen.

"If they even know when your birthday is." Jane.

"So they probably stick it on Christmas Day so's not to have to get you lots of presents," finished Linda.

They had gathered around me in a circle. They knew my mother was dead. They knew Grandma was in a hospital. I was fair game.

"If you get adopted, you'll be taken away and they'll change your name and we'll never see you again," Susan summed up. "Who knows where you'll go."

Patty had one more zinger. "You might become a maid." I saw her think about this. "Or maybe...maybe a slave!"

They made a new skipping rhyme out of it.

Apples, peaches, pears and plums.

Who cares when Cassie's birthday comes?

So Hazel thought Grandma should have got rid of me? I saw myself in a box on the front lawn, a baby wrapped in a pink blanket with a piece of paper pinned to my bonnet. *Please take. Free.* With kittens they write *Free to good home.* But I had the feeling Hazel wouldn't care.

Hazel had a mustache and hairs on her chin. And despite the fact I saw her take out her false teeth and rinse them after supper, her breath smelled like something was rotting in her dentures. I hadn't liked her before. Now I hated her.

CONNECTING DOTS

One day, lots of strangers came to my house.
Everyone dressed in black.
Told to go play at Patty's house.
I didn't connect the dots.

Chapter Four

Patty's mom was out and Patty had a babysitter. When Mrs. Huggins got home (in a black dress and a black hat), she said she was sorry my grandmother was dead. I told her she was wrong. "No, Mrs. Huggins. Grandma is in a hospital. You go to a hospital to get better," I explained to her kindly.

She looked annoyed and started to say something but she bit her lip. Really – she bit her lip. "You don't know, do you? I thought you were being a smarty-pants."

"Know what?"

Mrs. Huggins told me to sit down and she took my hand and she told me Grandma died two days ago. "I am sorry, Cassie. I truly am. We had our differences, but she was a God-fearing woman. And she took you in, despite people laughing at her behind her back."

Everything jumbled together. Grandma couldn't be dead. Couldn't be. And yet…it did all make sense, when I added things up. I remember being suddenly furious that she was gone and I hadn't been allowed to visit her…to say good-bye. But what was this other thing about laughing?

"Why did they laugh? What was so funny?"

Mrs. Huggins sighed and looked away. Then she said, "Oh H-E- double hockey sticks! *Someone* has to tell you." She played with her wedding ring a bit then she said, "When your mother – Rita – was in ninth grade, she was… well…a bit wild. Liked the boys a little too much and – Your grandmother took her away and stayed away herself for a few months. She came back and she told everyone that the child – you – was hers. We all suspected, of course. Shirley was just a teensy bit long in the tooth. Besides, I knew Rita. I babysat her sometimes. The boys sure loved her! Always coming around." She sighed again. "Well, your grandmother did the right thing by her own mind, and she's gone to her maker now. It isn't for me to judge." She settled back in her seat and looked like she was doing exactly that.

I didn't understand. "What did you suspect?"

Mrs. Huggins looked exasperated for a moment, then gave me a good up and down stare and seemed to realize she was talking to a seven year old.

"Oh, for heaven's sake! What have I let myself in for?" She started to titter but caught herself and instead said, "Cassie, you are illegitimate. Your mother got herself preg...with child, rather, and your grandmother pretended she was your mother because...well...Rita wasn't married. That makes you illegitimate."

Why did this silly woman look so pleased with herself?

I remembered something. "Ill," Patty had said. She told me I was ill and I thought she meant sick. But she meant this mysterious word *illegitimate.*

I remembered something else. "The other kids have fathers," I informed Grandma. "Why don't I have one?" Grandma got red in the face and turned her back to me. "Karen said I'm supposed to have one," I continued. Grandma put down the dishcloth and, not looking at me, said, "I don't know where your father is, Cassie, and that's the truth." I'd heard about lost children, but not about lost fathers. Grandma gave me a cookie and that was the end of it.

So I put it together with the logic of childhood. I was illegitimate because my father got himself lost, and if Rita couldn't find him she couldn't get married.

Now, looking at Mrs. Huggins, I whispered, "What happens to me?"

"Well, dear, I don't know. I expect one of your relatives will take you home with them."

Like a piece of furniture.

Some of what they'd said made sense all of a sudden, the whispered conversations I had overheard, the discussions – often angry – about tables and chairs and dishes and knickknacks.

They were dividing up Grandma's belongings and fighting over who got what. I had thought it very strange because when Grandma came home from the hospital, she would be fit to be tied if her house was emptied out.

"I don't know why you think you can march in here and take Grandma's belongings," I shouted. "You never came around before, not once. Not one visit. You didn't care about Grandma before. I don't even know you! Why – " I paused as it occurred to me. "Why, you could be anybody. Thieves, even."

Lana stared at me and muttered, "Any bickering over who gets *that*?"

Somebody's husband, I wasn't clear whose at the time, asked loudly, "Any booze in this house?" He opened a cupboard in the kitchen and held aloft a bottle of rye whiskey like he'd won a trophy.

I tried to grab it from him. “Grandma says it’s for medicinal purposes only.”

The man laughed. “Didn’t do her much good, did it?”

Chapter Five

They came back from the funeral. I was waiting on the front steps. "Why couldn't I go?" I asked, crying. "Why didn't you tell me?"

"Children don't belong at funerals," Hazel told me. "Too disruptive of a solemn occasion."

"But you didn't even tell me. I didn't even know Grandma was dead. Didn't she want to talk to me? Didn't she ask for me?"

"You think a great deal too much about yourself, Cass," Hazel said. "My sister didn't need to be bothered anymore with the likes of you while she contemplated her sins."

Grandma always told me to watch my mouth and mind my manners. "Particularly with old folks, Cassie. Old people don't appreciate wit and cleverness in a child. And you, the dear Lord knows, have an extra dollop of both."

I hoped Grandma wasn't listening, because I was about to let fly. "I know I'm ill… ill…illgitmat?" I heard the question mark in my voice and so said *illgitmat* more forcefully. "I know all about Rita. So there. I know Rita got herself preg-with-child (I remembered exactly how Mrs. Huggins had said it) because of lots of boys and I know she died. And I wish Grandma could have put me up for adoption before one of you lot gets your hands on me. So there!"

I was prophetic about them getting their hands on me because no sooner had I finished my speech, when I was ambushed from behind and flung over Great Uncle Ernie's knee. He hit me twice before I even realized what had happened. He hit me three more times before I heard Lana shouting.

"Dad! Dad! Stop it! That's enough!"

I felt her grab one arm and one leg and tug, and somehow I slithered off Ernie and fell to the floor. I saw his face – furious and red, with eyes bulging, spit flying – and I jumped up and ran down the hallway and into my room.

Slam!

I know there was a lot of commotion in the front room, but I decided this was a good time to howl – for Grandma, for myself, for Rita – and I didn't hear what they were saying.

It was dark before Lana opened my door and came in. She brought a sandwich and sat down. "You awake?"

I was lying on my stomach on my bed. "Yes," I mumbled.

"Hey, kiddo. I'm sorry about that. Dad hitting you and all. He gets a bit carried away when kids misbehave. I should know. He sure hit me enough when I was a kid!" She said it with a laugh as if she really thought it was funny – looking back on it as an adult. Ha, ha, ha.

"And I'm sorry about my Aunt Shirley dying. I know she was good to you. Never mind what Mom said. She's a little…old fashioned. But she is well-meaning, just like my dad."

I'd hate to see what ill-*meaning people were like.*

I turned on my desk lamp and looked at her.

"Why did you call me 'that'? You said, 'Any bickering over who gets *that*,' meaning me."

She sighed. "I know. It was rude. I didn't think. The question is, what's to become of you? You're kinda old to be adopted now. People who can't have kids want a baby. And besides, it wouldn't be right. People would talk. Mother would hate that. And part of the reason you never met any of us was because everyone (and she tossed her head toward the front room) was so mad at Aunt Shirley for taking you in, for pretending at first you were her daughter and not her granddaughter. Folks knew, Cassie, and they laughed. I remember my mom's reaction when she found out. Said she'd never talk to her sister again."

"So..." I swallowed hard. "What happens to me now?"

"Well, at the moment, it looks like Aunt Mabel and Uncle Fred are taking you. For now. Just to see how things go."

I felt sick. *Not them! Please not them!* And like a drowning person I grabbed onto Lana's arm, the one person who had been a bit kind. "Couldn't you take me? Please? I'll be good, I promise. And I'll work hard. At school, of course. But at home, too. I can do lots of things around the house. I know how to cook and clean.... You won't be sorry. I'll be good. *Please!*"

But even as I begged, I saw her eyes look away and she pulled her hand back, and I knew my hope was gone. The room seemed to tilt.

She pushed me down in the chair, and when the dizziness passed, I wanted to die...die and be with my mother and Grandma. It seemed like a good plan.

"I am sorry, Cassie. I truly am. But Dick and I are just starting out. We just got married, and our apartment is small, and it would be too hard for us. Really it would."

I guess she saw how desperate I looked, for she added, "But you could come visit us. Give everybody a break. We could go out, maybe see a movie, maybe go bowling. Get a pizza. Ever had a pizza? It's really good. *Eye-tal-yin* food, but still good."

Well, at least I wouldn't have to live with Hazel and Ernie. I don't know what I'd do if they came to stay.

Actually, I did know. If I couldn't die, I'd run away.

Chapter Six

Everyone except Mabel left the next day, with their cars packed to the brim with boxes and bags of loot. That's the way I looked at it – looters carting off whatever they could grab.

"Shirley would want me to have this," I heard many times. Or, "Shirley promised me this if...you know." "When? When did she say you could have that vase? I *know* she promised it to me."

And so on.

What about leaving stuff here for me to live with? At least no one stole the toaster and teakettle.

Fred left to go back to his job and Mabel stayed behind to take care of me. I wondered if Mabel minded not living with her husband anymore. If I were her, I'd be thrilled. He chewed tobacco and then spit the wad into a tin can. And he'd stick his finger in his ear and wiggle it around and then look at it to see what he pulled out. *Ugh.*

The next day, coming home from school, I saw a sign – FOR SALE – on our front lawn. And I wondered what Mabel was selling. Maybe the heavy dining-room set? The looters couldn't get that in a car.

By the end of the week, a sticker – SOLD – was stuck across FOR SALE. I went inside, expecting to see Grandma's furniture gone, but instead I saw empty boxes piled in a heap.

"You may fill two, Cass, and not one more," Mabel stated.

"With what?"

"Well, I'm sure I don't know. Whatever you think is important. But only two boxes, mind. Fred and I don't have a lot of room in our house for junk."

"Aunt Mabel? Why would I take my belongings to Uncle Fred's house?"

Mabel stopped folding towels and looked me over as if she'd never seen me before. "I'll tell you this much, Cass Jovanovich. When you're living under my roof, you'll watch your tongue and not be such a smart aleck. You know very well I've sold this house, and you're coming home with me."

Didn't see those dots at all. What a fool. I guess Patty's mom did say someone would take me home with them. Didn't pay attention.

I filled my two boxes with my best clothes and shoes and my Barbie doll. And Rita's photograph, of course – unstuck from my bureau and rolled up in the leg of a pair of tights until I could find another place for it. And I had a framed photo of Grandma and me from last year.

Mabel didn't let me bring any furniture from my bedroom. What she couldn't sell, she gave to the church.

Empty house. How big it seemed without Grandma's belongings.

I remember a moving van. I remember the backseat of Uncle Fred's Chevrolet. I remember getting to my knees to watch Grandma's house get smaller and smaller as we drove up the street.

There are a few other things. I don't really know where they fit. But I do know they belong to my life with Grandma. I want to leave them there with her.

My hair scotch-taped across my forehead so Grandma could cut my bangs,

Grandma knitting a popcorn sweater – white, with yellow duck buttons,

A first ride on the subway. Hiding my face in Grandma's skirt as the train rushed into the station,

A trip to Eaton's. Rubbing the brass toe for luck. Up the escalator, terrified I'd be sucked underneath the wooden slats,

A photo with Santa,

A picnic in Woodbridge. A new bathing suit – white stripes turned brown in the Humber River,

Feeding the deer in High Park and carrots in Grandma's pocket,

Grandma soaking off labels from tins of Campbell's Soup. A Campbell's Soup doll arriving in the mail,

Grandma giving me my very own record – "The Purple People Eater,"

Cutting out felt reindeer for my Christmas stocking with Grandma's pinking shears,

Reading in Grandma's lap,

Reading in Grandma's lap,

Reading in Grandma's lap.

Around the bend, and Grandma's house is gone.

Leanna is a fast reader, so why did she take so long to read my first bit of writing? I watched her face. Was it any good? Did she like it? She went back over some pages, and she smiled, and she frowned, and her mouth hung open at one

point. I thought I'd scream if she didn't hurry up! I went to the bathroom. I made tea. And she was *still* reading!!

Finally.

"I didn't know. I had no idea. This is so good! Wait! That's not what I mean! I mean, what happened to you is *awful,* but it's like a book. It is! I can't wait to find out…" She clasped her hands over her mouth and looked at me in horror.

"What you're trying to say, Leanna Mets, is you like my writing?"

She nodded. "Oh, yes! Gosh, yes! If it wasn't you, someone I love, well…"

The look in her eyes made me feel so proud. It was a strange feeling, not one I'm used to. "I'm going to write all Christmas vacation," I told her. "You ain't seen nothin' yet!"

Chapter Seven

The walls of the "guest room" were mustard-yellow. The quilt was dirty-brown. I lay on the bed like a hot dog.

"We don't have guests," Mabel said. She sounded pleased with herself. "No need to be wasting space setting aside a large room."

"Unless someone comes from the old country," Fred added. "But we don't encourage visiting."

The bed was tiny and squeaked when I moved. "Can we fix it?" I asked.

"Nope," Fred told me. "Like to know what you're up to."

There was a narrow desk and a wooden chair and a closet the size of a kitchen cupboard and a squat dresser with three drawers. I had to inch around it to get to the bed. There was nothing on the walls.

"Can we hang my picture of Grandma?" I asked.

"Nope. No nails in the walls. Might move one day. Don't want to be plastering and repainting."

"Besides," said Mabel, "we don't know how long you're staying."

That surprised me. "Aren't I adopted?"

They were as surprised as me and laughed. "What for? You're family. That should be good enough for any nosey parkers." I did not know what she meant.

They left me to unpack, and when I got off the bed – *squeak* – to close the door, Mabel was back in a moment. "You'll leave your door open. We'll have no goings-on in this house."

I didn't know what she meant by that, either. But I put my clothes away and Barbie on the bed and snuck Rita's photo out of my tights and slid it between the dresser and the wall. I put my framed picture on top of the dresser to one side and Grandma's hairbrush set in the center.

It was a miracle I had it.

"Shirley wanted Lana to have this," Hazel said one night, seeing it in my room at Grandma's house. She picked up the brush and comb, but before she could touch the hand mirror, I was out of my bed and lunging.

"Give me that! Put it down!" I screeched. "It's mine! Grandma gave it to me! She did!"

"She never!" Hazel replied. But I was on her and pulling, and when I screamed she let go of the brush and slapped me across the mouth.

"Behave yourself!"

Grandma never hit me and I was stunned. But only for a moment. I grabbed the brush off the floor and hugged it to my chest. "It's mine! It is! Grandma gave it to me when she was sick. When I combed her hair for her every day. She said I could have it when…when…when the time came."

The truth of what she meant by that was…she knew she was dying. She knew she wasn't going to get better.

I looked at the shepherdess on the back of the brush and cried.

"What's going on in here?" Mabel, standing in the doorway. Hazel began her claim all over again.

"Anton gave Shirley that brush set when they got married. You know as well as I do she'd never give it to Cass. Why, it might be worth quite a lot." She added, "Knowing Anton." She said it with a funny smirk.

Mabel. "I know no such thing, Hazel. It's a used brush and comb. If it means that much to Cass, then we should let her have something of Shirley's."

I did not understand why Mabel was being nice to me.

Hazel wasn't done. "Well, I never! You'd like that, wouldn't you? And her going to live with you. I'll be checking to see whose dresser it is on every time I visit. Just you watch me."

"Hazel May Hunter, you were always jealous that Shirley married Anton. Don't think I don't know *that.*"

"Huh! I thank the good Lord every day for sparing me the likes of that sod."

"Oh! As if he ever glanced in your direction! And as for visiting, don't be holding your breath, Hazel!"

I looked back and forth at them both and understood. It was like watching two girls fighting in the school playground. Mabel wasn't being nice to me – she was being mean to her sister.

I did feel smug now, as I arranged the set, some of Grandma's hairs in the bristles. I would never pull them out. If I held the brush to my nose and sniffed deeply, I could smell Grandma. And if I closed my eyes at the same time, I could pretend she was bending down to hug me, my nose buried in her soft auburn hair.

I held up the mirror. It was a little clouded, but it was the only mirror in this room.

Red hair in a ponytail. Blue eyes. Freckles. Three teeth missing. I wondered when I might start to look as pretty as Rita.

Supper was awful. Watery potatoes and pink chicken. Nobody spoke. We three sat at the plastic-covered kitchen table, as the clock went *tick-tock-tick-tock-tick-tock* till I thought I'd scream.

All meals were awful in this house. I offered some useful suggestions, but they were ignored.

Porridge every morning for breakfast. Mabel got up at five a.m. to make it for Fred who left by six to go to work in a factory. I got the cold, lumpy leftovers, stuck on the pot's bottom.

"Grandma let me put brown sugar on porridge. And Carnation Evaporated Milk. It tastes better."

"Porridge tastes like porridge. You'll eat what you're given."

And every morning – the dreaded ordeal. "Open up."

"No! What is it? It smells awful."

"Do as you're told. Open up, or else!"

So I opened up and Mabel shoved a spoon in my mouth and I gagged and swallowed the worst thing you could imagine. Dead, rotting fish.

"It's cod liver oil. A spoonful a day keeps the doctor away."

"I'll run away if I have to take this again!"

Smack! The spoon across the back of my hand.

"You are an ungrateful miss. After all we've done for the likes of you."

Off to school – a new school. The horror of starting three months late and standing at the front of the room to be looked over and judged.

"This is Cass Jovanovich. She's new here because she's come to live with a relative. Her parents are dead, and I know you'll all be nice to her."

Are teachers really that dumb? I was something weird and different. It started at recess with a new version of an old skipping song.

Cassie, Cassie took an ax, gave her parents forty whacks.

For how else could a mother *and* a father die?

"Was it disease? My mom said I shouldn't play with you. Maybe you're *con-tay-jus.*"

Cooties. I was a favorite "it." Cassie's Cooties became a new game.

Mabel had no imagination and sent me off every morning with that same tinned corned beef sandwich for lunch. I think when I complained before she must have bought a thousand tins out of spite. I never ate it. Anyone else who stayed at school for lunch got a much better meal than I did. Some even got little bags of potato chips and doll-sized boxes of raisins. I decided to start stealing lunch from others. I did this by putting my hand up every day around 11:25 to go to the bathroom. Then I swiped something from someone's cubby as I went by. Never the same cubby twice in a week. Never the whole lunch.

I had no idea I was such a good thief. I took a skipping rope one day and a pink tam with a tassel on another, just because I couldn't believe how easy it was.

My teacher wasn't really as stupid as I suggested. One day she followed me out into the hall – I guess I shouldn't have "gone to the bathroom" every day at the same time – and she caught me. I had stolen Marsha's new red mittens and was wearing them as I ate a cookie from Debbie's lunch.

Mabel was called to the principal's office. While I waited, Mr. Cozycabbage – no one could pronounce his real name – was nice to me. He suggested I was misbehaving because I missed my parents.

Mabel arrived. "Cass had a good Christian upbringing because of my sister. And I'll have none of it! None of it! There'll be no thieves in my house!" She hauled me down the hallway. I remember faces staring. There was pointing and giggling.

Then she muttered about my mother being a tramp. A tramp! I suddenly pictured Rita wearing raggedy clothes and carrying a stick with a bundle and jumping on and off railway trains.

Mabel had a ruler and she smacked my hands over and over. I was sent to my room. I didn't mind. I could smell boiled spinach again.

Last time she cooked spinach I wouldn't eat it. It sat there, this scoop of green-gray mush on my plate. I put a small bit on my fork, but halfway to my mouth the smell got to me and I knew I was going to throw up. I put my fork down. "I can't eat this," I said.

"Oh, yes you will. And you'll sit there until you do."

"Grandma didn't make me eat spinach. She tried, but she gave up. Even when I said I might be able to eat it from the tin like Popeye. I don't know how he does it. Spinach in the tin is worse."

Mabel didn't know much about Popeye. They had a television, but they only watched *The Lawrence Welk Show*. Sometimes they watched *Hazel* because it was about a maid called Hazel and Mabel made jokes about her sister. But no cartoons. At school, I couldn't talk about Captain Kangaroo or Mighty Mouse with the other kids.

"I don't care what nonsense my sister put up with. In this house, you'll eat your spinach, and you'll like it."

And so I sat there until nine o'clock until I had the brilliant idea of putting the spinach into the garbage and pushing it down deep. I showed Mabel my plate – with just a little bit left for a better lie – and she said I could go to bed.

The door flew open in the morning and Mabel was there with her ruler, trying to get at me. I jumped from the bed and leaped side to side, all the while hearing the *whoosh-whoosh* of the ruler slicing through air.

I was now a thief *and* a liar.

Nothing but shame and trouble.

I had to stay in my bedroom all morning. I got out the photo of Rita and asked why she went and died on me. Twice Mabel came in without knocking and asked who I was talking to. She even went over to the closet and yanked open the door.

I said I was saying my prayers.

"*Hmmmph!*" She didn't look convinced.

Chapter Eight

Mabel wanted me to stay in my room all weekend as punishment, but Lana arrived in the afternoon to take me out. She wasn't thrilled when her aunt told her I couldn't go.

"I came all this way, Aunt Mabel, and I don't care what she's done."

"I'll thank you to keep a civil tongue in your head missy, married woman or no."

"Aw, shucks, Aunt Mable. I didn't mean anything. Just...let her off the hook. She hasn't had an easy life. I'll get her back tomorrow by supper. Give you and Uncle Fred a break." Lana was a good wheedler.

"A break for what, I'd like to know," Mabel sniffed.

Lana dug Mabel in the ribs, playfully. "Aw jeez, Aunt Mabel. You're not *that* old!"

"You'll be keeping your nasty thoughts to yourself."

Lana laughed. I didn't know why. "Come on, Cass. Dick's waiting in the car." Then, in a stage whisper to me, "He can't stand to set foot in this mausoleum."

I got in the backseat of their car and felt like I'd escaped from prison. We drove down Yonge Street, and Dick honked his horn when we drove by the CHUM station, turning his transistor radio up high. Some song called "Hit the Road, Jack." I wished I could not come back to Mabel's no more no more no more no more, like the song said.

We went for pizza, just like Lana promised. Vesuvio's Restaurant was in a place called the Junction, and Lana and Dick had a fight because Lana said it was the best pizza, but Dick said they didn't serve booze. Lana won, but I don't know what the big deal was. Dick had a silver flask in his pocket and swigged from it whenever the waiter wasn't looking. The waiter brought a pizza to the table on a silver plate and cut it in slices, and after three weeks of Mabel's cooking I thought I'd died and gone to heaven. We had spumoni ice cream for dessert, like they do in Italy, and I wanted to move to Italy that very moment. The waiter pronounced it *Eat*-ah-lee and that made sense.

The waiter called me seen-your-Rita and kissed my

hand when we left. I wondered how he knew my mother's name.

We went back to Lana and Dick's apartment and watched *Hockey Night in Canada*. I saw a school yearbook on a shelf and began leafing through it.

And there she was – Rita. She was arm in arm with another girl, and when I peered closely, I saw that it was Lana.

Of course. Of course. Lana and Rita were cousins. Lana would know Rita. Of course! And they even went to the same high school. How dumb could I be?!

I turned to Lana, and she made a grab for the book, but I twisted away.

"You knew her, didn't you? You knew my mother. You could tell me about her, couldn't you? Couldn't you?"

She nodded. "Yes. I…I knew her."

"Pipe down!" Dick said, and he got up to turn the volume louder.

Lana looked at the ceiling and then seemed to make her mind up about something because she nodded her head again. "Come in here."

We sat at the kitchen table and opened the yearbook and found four pictures of Rita. In one she was wearing a tight sweater with those funny pointy bosoms. Underneath someone had written, *The Original Sweater Girl!*

Dick came in for another beer. He looked over our shoulders and whistled. "I'd forgotten how good she looked. Hot damn!"

"Dick!" Lana giggled. "You're terrible!"

Dick got his beer and then pointed a finger at my mother. "Well...sure explains everything now, doesn't it?"

"What does it explain?"

"Nothing. He's just being...male." Then Lana turned the pages and I saw a picture of my mom on the swim team, standing in a row of girls in front of a swimming pool.

"Where's that?"

"At our school. Humberside. We had an indoor pool. Rita was a good swimmer."

I studied the swim team. "How come her chest isn't pointy like in the other photo?"

Lana laughed. "Well come on. You don't wear a brassiere under a bathing suit."

She saw the confused look on my face. "In this photo," – and she stabbed at the original sweater girl – "Rita was wearing the new brassiere. Pointy tips. Like Jane Russell or Marilyn Monroe."

"Were they on the swim team?"

"They're movie stars, Dumbo!" She flipped to another page and I saw a photo of my mother at the prom. Junior princess! My mother was junior princess!

"Wow! Grandma said she was popular!"

Lana stared at the photo, and I think she was crying. "Yep. Junior princess in ninth grade."

"How did she die?" I whispered.

"Aunt Shirley didn't tell you?"

I shook my head. "She said when I was older."

Lana breathed out a sigh and it seemed to me she was relieved. "Well, then, that's what we'll do. I'll tell you when you're older." She jumped up. "Want some ice cream?"

I almost reminded her we'd just had ice cream at Vesuvio's but didn't bother. Not my fault if adults give me seconds of dessert. And besides, Mabel's idea of dessert was stale pound cake from the week-old section of the Dominion store bakery. *Ugh.*

It was boring vanilla, but Lana let me put BeeHive corn syrup on it.

"Christmas is coming soon. Ever go to the Santa Claus Parade?"

"Once. With Grandma."

"Well...want to go again? With me? Rita and I used to go. Even when we were older and didn't believe – "

"Didn't believe what?"

"Oh, um, didn't believe...that we should go. Too old. Little kids couldn't see around us."

"The time Grandma took me we got up early, but

I couldn't see anything around dads with kids on their shoulders."

"We'll go. I promise. Rita would like that. Me taking you."

Then it was time for bed and Lana let me sleep on the sofa and she gave me one of her own nightgowns because I was so excited to leave Mabel's I forgot mine. It was pale pink and lacy and I thought about trying to steal it and take it home.

Home.

I can't believe I ever thought of the hot dog with mustard as home.

Chapter Nine

I didn't go to the Santa Claus Parade.

This is what happened.

"What are you writing?" Mabel asked.

"My list for Santa. How do you spell *toboggan*?"

"I don't care what nonsense my sister put into your head in her house. In *this* house, we're God-fearing folks."

"Huh?"

She put her hands on her hips. "There is no such thing as Santa. It's time you learned what's what. And don't be thinking there'll be any gifts, either. It is a big enough gift having you here in our home."

No Santa?

"But what about my stocking? Grandma made it for me. We always hang it over the fireplace."

Fred piped up then, sticking his head around his paper. "No nails in the mantle."

"You're lying. You just don't want to buy any presents. Of course there is a Santa!"

Fred slammed his paper on the arm of the chair. Mabel went white. "I will not be called a liar. And in my own house! You are an ungrateful brat and…"

She was coming toward me, and I ran to my room.

I had the long, lonely evening to think it all through. Santa getting around the world in one night. Squeezing down everyone's chimney, even if the fire was lit. Santa carrying gifts for every kid in the world. Santa getting me everything I wanted. And then…when I found the Chatty Cathy doll I'd begged for in a box under Grandma's bed. It was under the tree Christmas morning, but until now…

Kids are dumb.

When Lana came the next week to take me to the parade, I refused to go. I told her why, and I heard her yell at Mabel. I couldn't catch it all, but I did hear, "Why are you always so mean? Huh? Why do you think Liz left home? Did you ever think about that? Huh?" A plate dropped and then there was more yelling and then Lana barged into my room.

"Come on. Forget the parade. Let's get out of here."

She asked me where I'd like to go and I said High Park. We bought carrots and I fed the deer like I used to. It started to snow and we ran across Bloor Street and ordered cola floats at a soda shop with stools that twirled.

"Listen. I know it's rough for you right now, kiddo. But don't worry. Christmas won't be so bad. I have a big secret. I could tell you, but..."

Slurp. "What? I won't tell. Promise." *Slurp.*

"Well...I guess if you're big enough to know about Santa Claus you're big enough to keep a secret. Right?"

Slurp. Nod.

"You can't tell Mabel and Fred." She leaned in and whispered as if Mabel and Fred were lurking nearby.

"Liz is coming home for Christmas. She hasn't told her parents. She wrote me a letter."

I didn't know anything about Liz. I knew there was a room in Mabel's house called *her* room. But it was always locked. Once I saw Mabel come out of it with sheets in her arms and although she pulled the door behind her, it didn't quite catch. When I heard the wringer going in the basement, I tiptoed in. There were photographs of a girl and teddy bears and dolls on the bed and school pennants hung on walls and cheerleader pom-poms hanging from the curtain rod. The room was pink and lavender and white lace, and I was bitterly jealous that I didn't have this room instead of the hot dog.

I heard Mabel plodding up the basement stairs and took off. I did not want to add *snoop* to *thief* and *liar*.

"Where is she? Why doesn't she live at home? Why is it a secret she's coming?" I demanded.

Lana looked the same as when I asked her about Rita. She sighed and said, "Well, let's see. Liz wanted a change. And a friend was going to California, so she hitched a ride. She quit her job at the bank and left her guy."

"So why's it a secret now?"

"Oh…. She isn't sure how they'll take it, so…she's doing a Christmas surprise. 'Tis the season and all that. Even Mabel and Fred should be jolly and loosen up a bit."

I thought of Mabel grunting to pull up her girdle – I didn't mean to snoop, but the door was open a crack one day – and she looked awful hot and sweaty. I didn't know how anybody so tightly squished could loosen up.

I had a tough three weeks, keeping the secret. So many times I wanted to tell Mabel and Fred I knew something they didn't, to make them mad, I think. But even more than that, I didn't want to let Lana down.

We were eating something Mabel called stew when the doorbell rang. And rang and rang and rang. Mabel and Fred looked annoyed, then angry as they tried to ignore it.

"Just a salesman," Fred declared. "He can ring till his finger falls off."

But whoever it was seemed happy to ring off all his fingers and finally they both got up to give whoever it was a piece of their minds. I used the moment to flush the stew down the toilet.

But in a flash I knew who it must be! I ran to see Liz in person.

She was hugging her mom, who seemed frozen and couldn't even manage to bring her arms up around her only daughter. Fred kept muttering, "Well. Well, I'll be. Well, I'll be."

I'll be what? I wanted to scream.

Then Mabel. "And you couldn't give a body some notice? Was your finger so broken you couldn't use the telephone? Well don't blame me if your room is filled with the dust of two years."

Liz just laughed out loud at them both. But I knew what a liar Mabel was – she dusted and cleaned Liz's room every other week. And I was about to say so, too, but then Liz saw me and stared.

"Oh, my. Oh, my stars. It's her. You're the spittin' image. Lana warned me but…oh, my." And she put a hand up to her eyes for a moment, before reaching out to pull me close.

She smelled wonderful and glamorous with a perfume

that bowled me over. The fur trim on her jacket tickled my nose and the cold air trapped in the fur brought something fresh into the stale air of that awful house. She took off her hat – really a bow on a band – and placed it on my head.

"We're going to have fun," she promised.

Chapter Ten

I remember coming home that last day of school before the holidays and smelling…cookies! Mabel never made cookies and Grandma hadn't for a long time.

Liz was in the kitchen dancing to music blaring from a small radio. She handed me a bowl and spoon and I took over dropping mounds of dough onto a cookie sheet. I scooped a glob into my mouth – oatmeal and raisins and coconut and pecans. Liz patted each one down with a fork and sprinkled miniature gumdrops on top.

"Grandma called these Gems," I told her happily. Somehow I felt thrilled we had this connection between us, even if it was just a recipe.

Of course, I was in love with her – Liz. Her dark hair and hazel eyes. Her tight pants and tighter sweaters and her string of pearls. Her shoes with "kitten" heels, she called them. The way she walked – shoulders back and bosoms out and her behind shifting side to side with each step. I had been practicing all week, but I knew I didn't look like her at all. Plus it was hard to see what I looked like from the back holding Grandma's hand mirror.

A song came on, a man singing about twisting. "Let's twist again," he begged, and Liz put down the bowl and grabbed my hands and spun me side to side like the wringer washing machine. Then we were down to the floor and up and down and Liz was laughing out loud and singing "like we did last summer," and I thought I might wet my pants I was laughing so hard.

The door smashed open and Mabel stood there in her coat, her chest heaving and her mouth pinched. She fumbled at the radio dial, but she grabbed the volume by mistake, and the song got louder, and so she gave up and yanked the cord out of the plug.

"In this house," she began, "in this house, *my* house, I'll thank you to remember – "

Liz cut her off. "Oh, I remember, all right. I remember everything." She picked up the cord. "I'm twenty-six years old. I'm home for a visit. It's Christmas. And you won't treat me like a child." She plugged the radio back in, but she turned down the volume.

Mabel stood there, not moving. I watched her, fascinated, even at seven wondering at the hate pouring out of her. Later that night, I imitated her face, trying to get it right, studying myself in the mirror.

Liz smiled then. "Come on, Mom. Loosen up." She held out a plate. "Have a cookie, for Pete's sake."

All Mabel loosened was her top button, but she did take a cookie. Then she marched out of the kitchen.

Liz winked at me, and when the silliest song came on, "Does Your Chewing Gum Lose its Flavor on the Bedpost Overnight?" both of us laughed out loud again.

I had no idea what was going on. When I was older, I heard someone say "you could cut the tension in the air with a knife," and I remembered Liz's visit home.

I pulled my decoration out of my schoolbag – dozens of red and green strips of paper looped together. Liz said we had to hang it up.

"Fred won't let us. Fred said no decorations. No nails or tape or – "

It was like waving a red flag at a bull. I saw the glee on Liz's face as she found the tape in the drawer and grabbed the step stool. I followed her into the living room and watched as she taped the garland to two walls, stringing it in front of the window.

Mabel watched us. "When your father gets home..."

Liz seemed determined not to let Mabel finish a sentence. "When Pops gets home, he can lump it." Then she looked around. "Where are we putting the tree?"

My heart leaped up! *A tree!* Mabel and Fred told me they wouldn't have any truck with any tree – real or fake.

Liz and I went to the church a block away and bought a tree from the Boy Scouts of Canada. We dragged it home through the snow, but we stopped at a hardware store to buy a stand first.

"We'd better get a string of lights and this box of ornaments, too," Liz said. "You can bet ol' Mabel and Fred won't have anything!"

I giggled. I loved the way she called her parents ol' Mabel and Fred.

We had the tree decorated before Fred got home, looking at us like we were thieves who'd broken in. Liz was flipping through a magazine and we were both eating cookies. I secretly rejoiced every time I saw a crumb fall on Mabel's floor. I crossed my legs the way Liz did and let my shoe dangle from my left foot like she did. This was how the Hollywood stars lived, I was sure.

But Fred didn't say anything about the tree. He glanced at it and then ignored it.

Liz went out most nights. Sometimes she walked, and sometimes we'd hear a honk and she'd go running out to a car. And when she left, it was like this big empty hole was left behind. I'd go to my room and read or color or do anything to avoid sitting in the front room with Mabel and Fred.

Ticktock, ticktock, ticktock.

But when Liz was home, or when Lana came and they took me out, I felt like the luckiest girl alive! They found me an old pair of skates and we went to an outdoor rink. They played music, and was there ever anything as magical as skating at night, under the lights, listening to "Take Good Care of My Baby" and "Runaround Sue"? They took me to see a movie – *101 Dalmatians*. They took me to see the windows at Eaton's and Simpson's. And Liz said, "We have to do something about your hair."

Mabel brushed my hair every day and yanked it into a braid down my back. It was so tight my scalp ached. Liz undid the braid and then began combing my hair the wrong way – from the ends to my head. Soon I had this fluff of red around my head like I'd stuck a finger in a socket. Then she smoothed some hair over the top and I had this big...kind of like a bowling ball on my head. She put a bow in it and said "Like it? It's called a beehive. Everyone in California wears it."

I loved it! I ran for Grandma's mirror and spent all night looking at myself this way and that.

Liz and Lana decided both families should eat Christmas dinner together. I heard Lana whisper, "That way I might be able to stand it!"

Mabel did her usual grumping. She didn't want to have a crowd in her house.

"Ma – it's your sister!"

And she didn't want to pull out the table and get out extra chairs and dust off the fancy plates and cook more than usual. And Fred complained about all the wasted money.

Liz ignored them and then Lana came over and I went shopping for groceries with them and they let me help cook.

Then it was Christmas Eve and Liz and Lana and some of their friends came and we all went to a church service. And there were candles and choirs singing and much to my surprise, there were kids my age acting out the nativity scene and talking out loud in church. How I envied them! Why didn't I know about this? Something rose up in my heart and I desperately wanted to be at the front, wanted to be the girl in the white angel costume with a halo tied in her hair. "Fear not! Glad tidings I bring to you…."

I went to bed that night, not with visions of sugarplums dancing in my head, but with thoughts of becoming a famous actress one day. I had one of Liz's magazines. Photos of Marilyn Monroe and Rita Hayworth and Elizabeth Taylor, who was a movie star when she was twelve. And I ripped out a picture of someone with a beehive so I could do it myself when Liz went away.

Because of course she would.

Chapter Eleven

Fred put his foot down when it came to hanging stockings from the mantel. But there were some presents under the tree. I couldn't believe there were four for me!

Liz took her time waking up, and she seemed a little unsteady on her feet. I noticed she had some mascara under her eyes, and her breath smelled funny when she hugged me. She wore a silky wrap that crossed in a V and it kept slipping open over her chest. I stole peeks at her tanned bosom and the little gold chain that hung there. This was glamor.

Mabel glared, her mouth pinched. "This is the Lord's birthday and I'll thank you to dress decently."

Liz yawned.

Mabel knit me a sweater as a present. I was shocked because she told me many times living with them was gift enough. I pulled it on over my head and saw the sleeves were too short.

"You'll have to add length," Liz said.

"I'll do no such thing. It's not my fault her arms are too long. Why, she's like a monkey with those arms!"

(Being called a monkey really hurt. A boy at school called me a monkey because I had hairy arms. So I shaved them. With Fred's razor. Mabel had a fit.)

Liz gave me a book about a girl called Nancy Drew and a new outfit for my Barbie and then...in the last box was a Ken doll! Barbie's boyfriend!

"It's just out," Liz said. "I went to three Sears Roebucks to get it and still had to line up."

"I love it!" I ran to my room and got Barbie and then I introduced her to Ken and made them kiss. Fred banged his fists down on the table and was up and across the room, grabbing Ken out of my hands.

"No!" he yelled. "None of that in this house!" He held Ken up over his head.

"Dad! Knock it off. You're being absolutely Victorian!"

Liz, Fred, and Mabel shouted about all kinds of things I didn't understand. I took Barbie and Nancy Drew and went to my room. Even the hot dog was better for the moment. I started reading Nancy Drew.

Liz knocked on my door – with Ken – and told me she needed my help in the kitchen. We put on music but Liz wasn't happy and hardly talked to me.

The others came and Dick opened a bottle of sherry. Even ol' Mabel and Fred and Hazel and Ernie had some. I snuck a bit and it was very sweet. We sat down, and Lana made us wear paper hats.

Dick carved the turkey and after only one bite I offered up my prayers of thanks. Delicious! Just like Grandma's dinners. And there were real vegetables and gravy.

Mabel complained. "Don't know why peas in the can aren't good enough for you. They're good enough for us."

"No they're not," I said. "They're awful!"

Lana hurried in to praise Mabel for her mashed potatoes. "Not one lump, Auntie!"

(Well, of course not. Earlier, I had watched Mabel whack the life out of those potatoes with the masher.)

But somehow, the dinner went wrong. No matter what anyone talked about, Fred and Mabel complained, and Hazel and Ernie joined in. The blow-up came when Liz talked about someone called JFK and how wonderful he was and how fashionable his wife was and how lucky she felt living in California.

Fred pushed back his chair and said, "That's enough. You think you can come waltzing back in here after the shame you put us through. You think you can talk nonsense about politics and movie stars and I don't know what all. But the day Americans voted in a Catholic president was a sad and terrible disgrace, and we won't talk about it in this house! Do I make myself clear?" And he stared at all of us.

Dick said, "Hey wait just a minute, buddy. You can't tell us what to think or do or say. Kennedy is doing a great job, and furthermore – "

"Get out! Get out now, the lot of you. I'll not have anyone eating at my table who thinks a Catholic president is a good thing."

There was silence, I remember that. And then Liz stood up. I thought she was going to shout, but she didn't. She was real quiet when she spoke. "I'll leave. I'll leave now, tonight. I'm glad I left two years ago. I'm not ashamed of who I am. And I'm glad I came back. It wasn't a misunderstanding back then, and now I know it for sure. You are dreadful people. Dreadful. And you can stick all your ignorant Irish prejudice right up your Blarney Stone!" She pushed back her chair and got up from the table, and then she said, "And you should be ashamed of your hypocrisy. You don't, any of you, go to church. *Any* church." She shoved in her chair and left.

Lana ran after her, and Dick sat at the table. He pulled

his flask out of his pocket and poured it into his ginger ale. The others didn't notice. They were staring at their plates.

I crept away and went to Liz. She was putting clothes into a suitcase and was still so calm. Lana was crying.

Liz paused in her packing. "I'm sorry, Cassie. I really am. I meant to stay for a few weeks. I meant to talk to you about...well...things. But I can't. I can't bear to be in this house one more day. I ran away before. I had to. They wouldn't let me be, wouldn't let me live my life. I had a boyfriend once and they...they acted as if I was a prostitute. They said the ugliest things. He was Italian and when they found out, well!" She looked at Lana and they smiled at each other. "They come from a dark and ugly place. The world is changing, Cassie. People like me want to let go of old ideas and prejudices, and people like my folks want to cling to a past of remembered insults and hate. It's what they live for."

I couldn't stand it. "Take me with you."

"Oh, honey. I wish I could. But I can't just take a minor across the border. There's so much paperwork and legal..."

She saw the expression on my face and took pity. "But you could come visit.... Maybe this summer. I'll see to it, I promise." She looked at Lana. "Maybe you could come, too. Bring Cassie with you. You'd love San Francisco. So much is happening there."

There was a pause and a look went between them and then Lana said, "Sure! That's a great idea. How 'bout it, Cass? You and me on a road trip?"

I knew a cue when I heard one. "You bet!" I said, knowing that it wouldn't ever come true.

Chapter Twelve

Liz left Christmas night. She hugged me. She said she wouldn't forget me. She said she wanted to tell me about Rita. She said, "No matter what you hear, don't listen to them. Promise?"

I promised, but *what* I promised wasn't clear.

Dick and Lana went with Liz. Fred pulled down the tree and threw it outside, lights and all. Mabel banged about in the kitchen. I stayed in my room and wished, like Nancy Drew, I could escape in my roadster and take off after crooks.

In the morning I saw my garland hanging out of the garbage can, red and green dye on the snow.

I would not have believed life could get worse. But after

the thrill of Liz, everything seemed awful. Mabel and Fred barely spoke to each other, let alone me. One day I realized Mabel was sleeping in Liz's room and not with Fred. One night I was sure I heard her crying.

I didn't want her in Liz's room. She didn't belong there. And I wanted it for myself.

I stole again. Bits of lunch like before, but sometimes books or toys or pieces of clothing. This time I was careful to stick one or two items into other kids' pockets. What a thrill when some poor fool got caught. Mrs. Lane gave me a funny look sometimes, but I just stared right back. Innocent.

No one remembered my birthday, March 16. So I stole a Twinkie from Patsy and I stole a Nancy Drew book from Sandy.

After school, I snuck into Liz's room and took a frilly nightgown from her drawer. I didn't write *steal* because I was sure Liz wouldn't mind. Then I had a party for myself in my room and ate my Twinkie with Rita and Grandma watching me.

One night Fred didn't come home for supper. He wasn't home when I went to bed. Fred never did come home again. The police found him in a ditch not too far away. Dead. His car was crashed up. They think he had a heart attack and swerved.

This time I got to go to the funeral. It was very small and I didn't know anyone except for family. There were other family members there, but I didn't know them. They stared at me, and I stared right back. Liz didn't come home. She sent flowers, but I saw Mabel take them from the stand by the casket and bring them home. I thought she was being sentimental, but later I found the vase smashed in the garage and the flowers – yellow daisies – thrown on the compost heap at the back of the yard. I picked one daisy that wasn't crumpled and placed it between the pages of Nancy Drew.

Strangers came back after the funeral and got very drunk. Some really old women came in a group and sat wailing. It gave me the creeps, and I stayed in my room.

Life got better. Even though her husband was dead, Mabel was less dreary. She bought Carnation Milk for our porridge and sometimes she even bought Alpha-Bits cereal! She let me cook sometimes and was a bit chattier, telling me stories about growing up with Hazel and Shirley.

I found out she and Hazel were about twenty years old when Shirley was born. Home was Hilltown, County Down, Northern Ireland. (Coontie Doone, she said.)

"There were four of us, but our brother died young."

Another great uncle? "What was his name?"

Mabel laughed, except laughing for her was such an unusual thing, I don't think she knew how. She kinda wheezed, as if she'd run a race and couldn't breathe properly. Her lips curled up a bit, that's how I knew.

"Mother sent us off a day after to register the birth. Alfred Joseph his name was. But Hazel swore it was Joseph Alfred. They were fed up with us arguing and registered him alphabetically. Alfred Joseph. Hazel never forgave me for getting my own way."

She wheezed out another chuckle and wiped her eyes. "But then Alfie ups and dies so it didn't matter a-tall. Shirley came along years later when mother should have known better."

Mabel and Hazel left Ireland for Toronto hardly knowing Shirley, my grandmother. They took her in when she came over and then she met Anton Jovanovich and got married. Mabel and Hazel looked to be heading for "old-maidhood," but then they met Fred and Ernie at a dance and got married and had Liz and Lana a couple of years before Rita was born. I stuck in a few questions about my mother, but that always made Mabel seem to notice me and stop talking.

In May she told me to sit down. She had something to say.

"I'm selling the house," she said. "I'm moving back to

Ireland. I've got cousins there and I've a fancy to see the old country again."

Ireland! I jumped up and did a jig.

"When do we go? Will I finish second grade?" I was already thinking about how I'd tell the kids at school.

Her body stiffened, and in a split second, all the traces of kindness and the little hope I had for my future were gone.

"You? You're not going, you dimwitted girl. No one is interested in having anything to do with the likes of you. There's enough shame and trouble there already without importing some of it back."

How stupid of me. I don't know how I finished the school year. I don't know how I slept or ate or played with the other kids.

Because in August, I was going to live with Hazel and Ernie.

Leanna put down the last sheet of paper. She looked up at me, but she didn't say anything.

"Not what you expected, huh?"

She shook her head. "No. No it isn't." She reached for my hand. "You don't have to keep going. You don't. I'm sorry I made you do it."

"You didn't *make* me. You suggested it. And the truth is, I don't mind. It's not pretty stuff, but I don't mind. I don't. I actually kinda like it. It feels like...sort of like..."

"*Catharsis!* That's the word you want! *Catharsis* means...a release. An emotional release and you feel better because you let go of something painful. You can look it up in the dictionary."

"I don't have to, now." I grabbed a pillow and hit Leanna over the head. Again and again. She found her pillow and hit me back. And we were yelling and knocking things over and Mary knocked on my door.

"All right in there?" she called.

I smiled. "Yup! Everything's groovy," I yelled, as I sat on Leanna and tried to suffocate her. She pushed me off and managed to grab my foot and tickle, which wasn't fair because she knows I have terrible ticklish feet.

Then it was over and we lay panting on my bed and I told her, "Christmas brought it all back. I remembered so much, and I remembered how I felt, and I had to write it."

"Will you keep going? I mean, now I know that novels about orphans and...and such...make it seem glamorous and fun, and it's not. So you don't have to keep writing."

I shrugged. "We'll see. I'm pretty busy right now. I've got a lot of lines to memorize. We have Kids for Kids practice twice a week until the show. And I have my Speech

Arts exam too. At the Royal Conservatory. I have to recite bits from two plays and a poem. Want to hear?"

I jumped off the bed and took a deep breath. "That's diaphragm breathing. Actors have to learn how." Then I began with "The Highwayman."

The wind was a torrent of darkness among the gusty trees.

The moon was a ghostly galleon tossed upon cloudy seas.

"You sound funny," Leanna said.

"Because I'm enunciating. You can't mumble or drop your consonants, or they won't hear you in the back row." I did the rest. Then I did Joan of Arc from *The Lark* and then Frankie from *The Member of the Wedding*. When I finished, Leanna was glowing.

"You're wonderful! You sounded so aristocratic and then just like someone from the south. Just like in *Gone With the Wind!* My gosh!"

I grabbed her hands. "Really? You really think so? You're not just saying that?"

"No. I mean it. Boy oh boy! Man oh man! That's a neat line. I'm going to use it, sometimes."

"I like your hair," I told her. Her bangs were growing out and her hair was shorter and she wore a headband and her hair curled around it. And she had new glasses, too. "You look pretty, Leanna."

She blushed. "Ever since my mom got a job at Simpson's she lets me use her discount and shop by myself. She even let me get TK Cords! And she doesn't bother with me like she used to. She's busy now and gives me an allowance and jobs to do in the apartment."

"That's what it's like here, too. Peter and Mary teach sociology at the University of Toronto. That's the study of how human society works. Our institutions and such. But Mary and Peter say our institutions don't work. They complain about the establishment and say *anti-establishment* and *status quo*, whatever that means. But they give me money every week, and I do stuff around the house.

"And there's always people invited over. Students and other professors. And they argue about everything. I don't know what they're talking about. War. Peace. Vietnam. Rights. Civil rights. Women's rights. I try to listen because they keep asking me what I think. I get a headache. Everyone used to tell me to shut up and mind my own business. Peter and Mary ask me what my opinion is. I try to pay attention so I can sound smart."

Leanna hugged me. "I'm so happy for you Cassandra. It's all worked out, hasn't it?"

She sounded so wistful. She wanted so badly to think I was finally happy. Well, I wasn't *unhappy*, just, still, a bit… unconvinced this could last. Mary might change her mind and off I'd go again. Hey kiddo! Here's some new clothes, and go get your suitcase!

Speaking of which, I showed Leanna the new clothes Mary and Peter got me for Christmas – a mini-skirt and a mock turtleneck sweater and heavy tights and desert boots. Then I showed her my new prized possession.

"A transistor radio?! Really? You lucky, lucky girl!"

Yeah. That's me. A lucky, lucky girl.

Peter came home with a pizza and we watched *The Ed Sullivan Show*. We fell asleep with the transistor on and the batteries wore out and the last song I heard was "The Sound of Silence."

Hello darkness my old friend....

Chapter Thirteen

Hazel and Ernie didn't want me. Mabel and Fred hadn't wanted me either, but this was different. Mabel and Fred took me on as some sort of Christian duty, or so they said many times. They made it clear there was something wrong with me because of Rita, and I wasn't happy living there, but I wasn't afraid either.

I don't know when I became afraid at Hazel's. I didn't have my own bedroom. I slept on a couch in Hazel's sewing room and I had to put away my blanket and pillow before I left for school. I kept my belongings in my suitcase and I covered it with a throw from Mabel's. But sometimes when I came home from school, I knew one of them had looked through it. It gave me the creeps.

I asked Lana to keep my brush set. I didn't trust Hazel.

Sometimes I'd look up and see Ernie watching me. I felt sick. I didn't know why. I'd see Hazel watching Ernie and then she'd flick her glance over to me – a glance filled with suspicion. My stomach knotted and I couldn't swallow.

At school one day I got into a fight with John Rait. He was reading The Hardy Boys. I knew they solved mysteries like Nancy Drew. I asked if I could read it after him.

"No. You can't. You're a girl. Girls can't read The Hardy Boys. You're only allowed Nancy Drew."

I punched him at recess. I caught him at the four-squares game and pushed him down and punched his head into the concrete.

The principal called "home."

Ernie came. I don't know why he was home in the afternoon, but he smelled funny – like Liz did on Christmas morning. I saw the principal sniff the air, but still, he sent me "home" early with Ernie.

Ernie put me over his knee. He pulled up my dress and he pulled down my underpants. I struggled – horrified – and tried to pull my underpants back up. He slapped my hand. Then he hit me over and over. I bit my lip. I would not cry. I would *not* cry.

"Come on, little miss. Cry or else. Cry or I'll not be stopping."

Five more times he hit me.

I cried. My teeth clenched, my lips tight, I sounded like an animal grunting.

"Ah. There it 'tis. There it 'tis." He left his hand on my bare bum. "I hope that learns you. No misbehaving in my house. Bide me now." He pushed me off.

I couldn't take my eyes off his mouth – smiling. Thin lips pulled back from stained brown teeth. I couldn't move.

He gave me a quarter. "Best not say anything to your aunt. No need to upset her. No need for her to know about your misdeed at school. You're a good lass. Run along now."

At supper I couldn't sit.

Hazel. "What's the matter with you? Sit down!"

Ernie watching. I said nothing. I pushed into the floor with my heels and kept my body an inch off the chair.

One night Ernie didn't come home. We ate supper and he still wasn't home. I hoped he was dead like Fred. Smashed to bits in a ditch. Rats eating his brains.

I saw him coming down the street, his balance off. He stumbled up the steps and crashed open the front door. The stupidest grin on his face.

Hazel. "Where have you been? As if I didn't know."

The grin was gone. Ernie staggered and fell. Got up. Looked into the kitchen. Saw the supper plate on the table. He frowned and tried to sit down.

"What's this? What's this mess? Not fit for a dog." He threw the plate at the wall. He pushed back his chair. It fell over, tangling him up, and he stumbled again.

"Stupid. Stupid hag." He threw his arm out and swiped the crockery off the kitchen counter. All of it broken on the floor. Sugar, flour, salt, coffee. All on the floor.

He pushed past Hazel and he moved to the cellar stairs. I heard him go down. *Fall and break your neck!*

I looked at Hazel and let out my breath. I didn't know I'd been holding it.

"Go on then. Stop staring and go to bed."

Ernie was late two more nights. Hazel didn't leave any supper out. He stumbled in, looked around, and swore. Then he went downstairs.

There was a couch in the cellar. Old and stained. I crept down to look one day when I got home and Hazel wasn't around. The room stank – an unwashed blanket and dirty clothes. I saw an empty bottle of rye and I saw a puddle of something spilled. A toilet in the corner was almost overflowing with unflushed urine.

I gagged and ran upstairs. I ran out of the house and down the street to the park. I swung and swung and wished to fly off into the clouds.

I went to visit Michael. He lived around the bend and he was born with what everyone called a "condition."

His heart was outside his body. I didn't believe this when Christine told me, but it was true. He had a bump on the outside of his chest. If his mother wasn't around, he'd let us touch his heart for a dime. I cupped my hand over the bump and felt his heart beating like a baby bird's. Michael was very pale and didn't go to school. His mom and sisters taught him at home and a nurse came every day.

Michael thought he was very special because he wasn't going to live much longer.

I envied him.

On the fourth night, Ernie came home with flowers and a box of Lowney maraschino chocolates. He went down on one knee and begged Hazel to forgive him.

"You're a darlin' and I don't deserve you. If you'll forgive me, my sweetheart, I'll never touch a drop again. I swear on me dear mother's grave."

Hit him. Take the frying pan and smash it over his head.

Hazel. "Get up you silly fool!" Simper. "I know you'll do your best. I know you didn't mean it. It's the rye, it is and not your fault a-tall."

Then Hazel, humming in the kitchen, making supper. Happy. Smiling.

Ernie in the living room, calling for tea.

"Go on, then. Take your uncle his tea."

I carried the mug. I stretched out my arm and placed it on the table beside him. I stepped away.

He was too fast for me. He grabbed my hand and pulled me onto his lap. I squirmed and he held me tight.

"Shhh. Shhh, now." And he bounced me up and down. Up and down. Up and down.

He pushed me off, suddenly. He reached into his pocket and gave me a quarter. He winked.

One day I took Hazel's dentures to school for show and tell. They sat in a glass of water every night, and she put them in when she woke up. But I had been watching Charlie McCarthy and Mortimer Snerd on TV. I made a puppet at school and thought Hazel's dentures were the perfect final touch.

I gave a great performance. Hazel was furious. She'd been all day without her teeth. Over supper, she told Ernie how bad I'd been.

"There's a wickedness in her, father. Wickedness. I know how she come by it, and I know how I'm going to flush it out."

That night she took me into the bathroom and closed the door. She pulled a box from under the sink and in it was a bit of hose with a ball at the end of it. She filled the ball with water and said, "On your knees with you."

She shoved me and pulled my shorts and underpants down. She pushed and poked and then the hose was in my bum. She kept one hand on my back, holding me down, and she squeezed the ball end until I felt hot water surging into my body.

I let out a yelp and thought I was going to explode. I heard a funny gurgle and Hazel heaved me onto the toilet. The water and everything else surged out of my body in a rush of stink.

She stood there, arms crossed, nodding. "Sit till you're done. Then clean yourself up."

After that, whenever I misbehaved – no matter what – Hazel brought out the enema – that's what the box called it.

I lived there for all of grade three and into grade four, and every few weeks Ernie stumbled up the steps to the house.

She always forgave him, blaming it on the awful men he worked with in the factory.

One night I was asleep, and suddenly I wasn't. My heart was pounding. Someone was in the room. Someone was inching closer. Then I smelled him. The terrible stench of him. Not down in the basement, sleeping off the drink. Here.

He sat down on the couch and put his hand on my back. He rubbed me up and down. He tried to turn me over, but I went stiff and wouldn't move.

I didn't make a sound.

He went away.

I went to sleep every night after that clutching a pair of Hazel's knitting needles. I lay there, listening for any sound...every sound. One day, I went to school, and we had a test, and I threw up on the sheet.

Please don't call home. Please don't call home. "I'm fine. Really. I'm not sick."

Once we had a short day for some teacher meeting. I came home, and the door was unlocked. I knew Hazel was at a doctor's appointment.

I heard splashing. The bathroom door was open.

He was naked. Lying in the tub. One leg splayed over the side. His eyes were closed and he was humming.

I backed out. I could not make myself turn around. I backed all the way to the front door, and then ran to Christine's house. Her mother was home and I begged to stay.

"Well, really Cass, I'm getting supper ready and Christine has homework. You should go home."

I shook my head. "I can't. I...I..." Inspiration struck. "I think there's burglars. I think someone's inside. The door was open, and my aunt's not home, but I heard something and..."

Christine's mother picked up the phone and asked the operator for the police. She told them what I'd said. She gave them my address. Then we went outside to wait and watch.

What had I done?

The police came. They circled around the house. They went inside. I don't think I breathed for five minutes.

They came out and called me. Christine and her mother came, too. Ernie was in his housecoat, and he was mad.

The police thought it was funny, but they told me to be more careful about wasting their time.

Hazel arrived and couldn't take it all in. I was home early and Ernie was home early and the police found Ernie in the bathtub. She glared at me and told Christine's mother to go about her own business.

"Well! I never!" Christine's mother replied. But she dragged Christine away and I could hear her telling her to stay away from "our sort."

Our sort. As if.

Then I was suddenly alone with Ernie.

"But you saw me, didn't you, my girl?"

I shook my head. *Not your girl!*

"In the bathtub."

"No…no. I…no. Never."

"I saw you watching me. A man in the privacy of his own bath. I saw you look. And now you'll be lying on top of that? *Tsk.*"

He winked at me. I choked back the vomit in my throat.

"And then you thought to call the police." He shook his head. "Naughty girl. Naughty girl. Won't have that in this house, I won't. I'll have to be teaching you another lesson."

He smiled at me with those awful yellow teeth. Yellow from years of smoking those stinky cigarettes he rolled in the basement. Licking the paper with his fat tongue, peering at me over the top of his glasses.

Two days went by until Hazel was out and I was alone with him.

"Come here, lass."

I tried to get by him. I did. The front door was there. So close. I couldn't make my legs move.

"Come along now. I won't hurt you. You know it doesn't hurt. Why, I seem to remember you enjoyed it. Didn't you now?"

Arm out. So fast. His hand on my wrist. Pinching. Pants down. Underpants down. But this time...this time he'd undone his belt.

He saw the fear on my face.

"Oh, now, don't be worrying. You're too young for the belt. 'Tis the hand for you, yet."

He pulled me onto his legs.

Smack. Smack. Smack. Rub. "Rub a dub-dub. It doesn't hurt now, does it? Eh? Say it doesn't hurt."

"Does...doesn't."

"What? Doesn't what?"

"Hurt. Doesn't."

"Good lass. Good lass."

Smack. Smack. Sm –

Neither of us heard the door open.

"Dad!"

I was on the floor. Pushed. Banging my head on the chair leg.

He grabbed at his buckle. "It isn't – "

"Shut up! Shut up!" Lana screamed. She slapped him.

She found my hand and pulled me up. "Here. Get dressed. Hurry. I knew it! I should have known! I should have! I did! I can't believe – "

She kept screaming, and her father didn't move. "Get your clothes. Get whatever you can. Hurry up. We're leaving. Hurry, Cassie."

Then she spit in her father's face.

And we were out the door.

I had jumbled everything I owned into Mabel's throw and run out of the house like a hobo.

Weeks later, I emptied out my tin can of quarters. There were fourteen. Fourteen quarters. There should have been fifteen. I bought a Lowney Cherry Blossom. But I choked on it. I could not swallow it. "Nora said someone once found a worm in the cherry." That's what I told the kids with me when I bought it and threw it away.

I gave the rest of the quarters to Michael for the privilege of touching his heart.

Chapter Fourteen

"I won't go back."

They sighed.

"I won't. I won't! I'll tell. I'll tell the school. I'll tell the police. I will."

"Now honey – "

"No. *No!*"

"But tell what? Dad says he was just punishing you for misbehaving. That's all."

All.

"You don't believe that. You can't. You hit him. You spit at him. You – " And I knew. *I knew.* "He did it to you too, didn't he? Growing up. Didn't he?"

Lana crossed her arms and rolled her eyes. "Listen, Cass –"

"How many times? How many quarters did he give you? Huh?"

Lana went to her bedroom and slammed the door.

"Oh, for Pete's sake," mumbled Dick.

He went after her. He closed the door and I could hear them.

Arguing about me.

Well.... I said before I'd run away, and so I would.

Dick came out first. "Listen. She's pretty upset with, you know, everything you've said about her dad."

I started to protest and he interrupted me. "But wait a minute. Wait a minute. Don't worry. You can stay here for a while. Until we sort things out. Okay? Deal?"

I wanted to relax. I wanted to believe him. "For how long? I'm just a kid. You can grab me and haul me back there, and what can I do about it?"

Dick smiled. "Oh, I think there's plenty you'd do about it." He sat down. "Cassie, I believe you. I do. Lana has told me things. Not much, but enough. And I'm not stupid. I know what goes on. Nobody wants to admit this stuff, but, man, the lid's going to blow soon, I tell ya."

I wasn't sure what he meant, but he seemed to be on my side.

"Cassie, I don't know how we'll fix this, how we'll manage, but we will. Okay?"

I nodded.

"Come on. Sit down." He patted the couch beside him.

I sat down in the rocker. He looked at me funny.

"Listen. I don't know exactly what went on. But I hate the guy – Hazel, too. Why, she must be hell on roller skates to live with! When I met Lana, I fell head over heels. When I met her folks, I almost broke it off. I don't know how someone so sweet came out of that house, that's for sure."

"What...what did she tell you?"

"Aw...I don't know. Just...let's not talk about it, okay? Makes me sick, to tell you the truth." He looked up at the ceiling, then over at me. "Want to know something else? I was real sorry when your grandma died. A good woman. Know what I mean?"

Of course. Of course I know. I started to sob. Big, blubbery sobbing. Not clenched teeth grunts.

"I'm sorry, Cass. And we'll work it out. I promise. Cheer up, okay?" He handed me the box of Kleenex.

Behind me, Lana came out of the bedroom. "I'm sorry, hon. I really am. I've...I've got stuff, you know? It goes back. And...they're my folks, you know?"

I didn't know. I didn't have "folks." But I nodded and said I'd help with supper. I cleared the table after and washed the dishes and swept the kitchen floor.

Dick set up a camp cot in the hallway by the front door. I lay down and was surprised when I saw it was morning. I didn't think I'd be able to sleep. Maybe it was the first time in weeks that I wasn't scared. Not clutching knitting needles.

Dick drove me to school that day. I didn't want to go, but Lana said she phoned her mom and told her I needed a break from routine. "Mom didn't even ask why," I heard her say to Dick.

I was terrified to get out of the car. What if they were there, waiting to drag me back? But I didn't see them all week, or the next week, either. No one seemed to know anything was different, not even the teacher. Nobody asked any questions about where I was living. So I began to relax. And I didn't steal or cheat or fight in the playground.

That first Saturday Lana took me shopping. "Those clothes have to go," she said, shaking her head. "Where'd you get them?"

"Rummage sales."

We went to a plaza near the apartment to a store called Chic Casual. I thought it was *chick*, like a chicken, but I heard the saleslady say "*sheeek*." Her hair was in a bun and she wore really high heels that clicked when she walked. She wore a tight skirt and a tight sweater. I wanted to look like her. I vowed that someday I would.

Lana bought me two pairs of jeans and three tops and a dress in something called paisley print. We got runners and a pair of patent leather dress shoes. She took me to the hairdresser and Pino trimmed my bangs and cut off about six inches of split ends. He shook his head the whole time and pursed his lips. But he did say my color was *magnifico*.

One day, Lana said I was old enough to take the bus home from school. Dick didn't mind dropping me off in the morning, but it would be better if I got home on my own. Lana gave me a dime every day for my ticket and I felt so mature, so much worldlier than the other kids. It killed me, but I didn't say anything. I didn't want to draw attention to myself. If someone blabbed to her mom, and then her mom blabbed to Hazel – What if she said I was too young to take a bus? What if she demanded I go "home"?

My teacher, Mrs. Workman, said I was looking very good. "I'm so glad, Cass. Really. You were looking a little… neglected?" I knew she was trying to ask me something, but I played dumb.

I kept to myself. I offered to clean the blackboards at recess every day so I could stay inside in case Hazel came to the school at recess and called me over to the fence. What if she made a scene? What if the principal told me to go home with her? What if I couldn't refuse? What if, once again, I could not make my legs run?

But two weeks passed and nothing happened. Today was November 22, and soon it would be Christmas, and I began to hope. Why, maybe Liz would even come back and stay with us at Lana's!

It was afternoon recess and I used the shammy on the board to get it really clean, and I heard the teacher come into the room. I turned around. Her face looked terrible.

I knew it! It's them! "What…what is it, Mrs. Workman?"

"The president. He's been shot. Killed. JFK. President Kennedy. He's dead."

She started to cry and she fumbled for a chair – a little kid's chair – to sit on. I remember thinking how odd it was – her knees up to her chin and her so low down.

JFK! Liz's president. What would Liz be thinking? I remembered the picture I had torn from a magazine. JFK and his beautiful wife, Jackie. I had a collection of pictures, now that I knew about them. It connected me to Liz, to the make-believe that some day Lana and I would get in a roadster and go on a trip to California.

I took the bus home after school and people were outside, arm in arm, weeping. The news was everywhere.

Lana and Dick were having a party the next day and

didn't know whether to cancel it or not. It was like someone they knew was dead.

They went ahead, and I helped, putting ice in glasses and handing around bowls of nuts and bolts. If everyone said I was useful, Lana might keep me.

People came in quiet. They all said the same things. Lana cut out a photo from the newspaper and taped it to the wall and everyone said something about Camelot. But pretty soon people were having second and third drinks and someone told a joke. Then Dick raised his glass and said that the good always die young.

"Like my mother, Rita," I said.

A woman I didn't know swiveled around to stare. "Rita's dead? When? I just saw her last week!"

A glass smashed in the kitchen.

Chapter Fifteen

Silence.

People either looked at me, or the kitchen doorway.

Someone in the bathroom flushed. A woman giggled and a man hiccupped.

I found my voice. "What do you mean? What do you mean you saw my mother?"

Another woman said, "Rita's your mom? No kidding!"

I thought I would go crazy. Lana came out of the kitchen. "Not now, Cassie. Okay? Later, I promise."

"Promise what? To tell me why my mother is or isn't dead?" I was shrieking. Dick grabbed my arm and pulled me down the hall. He flicked the dial on the record player as he went by and music blared.

Dick pushed me onto their bed. "Quiet. Just be quiet. You heard her. She said she'd tell you, and she will. But not in front of everyone, you hear me? We're not gonna ruin the party on top of everything else." He went to the door. "You're going to stay in here. Watch TV. I'll bring you some food." He was out with the door closed before I could answer.

My thoughts were all over the place. Was I mad because my mother wasn't dead? Or was I mad she was alive? Or was I mad because I felt like an idiot?

Dick came back with a box of chips and two bottles of Orange Crush and a bowl of Bridge Mixture. "Here. Knock yourself out."

I turned on the TV and adjusted the rabbit ears, but it was all stuff about JFK or Lawrence Welk. *Yuck.* So I snooped around the bedroom. I found a box of magazines called *True Crime* in Dick's side of the closet. Lots of gory pictures of dead women in negligees or half-naked, and tough-guy cops making snarky comments. Pretty sure I wasn't supposed to be reading this.

Sue me.

I ate everything and felt sick and thought about throwing up on their bed. I guess I fell asleep, because in the morning I was on my cot in the hallway. The living room was a mess. I could hear Dick snoring but Lana was on the sofa, still in her dress, staring out the window. I sat in the swivel chair and swung it back and forth until she stuck out her foot and jerked me still.

"She isn't dead. Aunt Shirley told us she died giving birth to you. Then Rita wrote us letters – Liz and me – and told us the truth. The three of them made us go along with it. Shirley, Hazel, and Mabel. They said it was for the best. For you." She picked up a glass and sniffed, made a face, and drank. "Liz and I hated them. Hated having to pretend our cousin was dead." She finally looked at me. "We loved Rita."

I didn't move. I was afraid of stopping this flow of information.

"If our mothers found the letters, they destroyed them. We tried something else – a post office box – but after a time...well, I guess Rita moved on. She sent a couple more letters from Detroit and New Orleans and then...nothing. And I guess that might have been it, if your grandmother hadn't died." She poured some fresh vodka into her glass. "So. Any questions?"

As if she'd just explained some arithmetic to me.

I cleared my throat. "Why?" I began. "Why...."

"Oh, come on, Cassie. You're almost ten. You're not naïve. Rita got pregnant. She was sixteen when you were born. Don't you know how people would talk? So off they went, and Rita had you in a home for unwed mothers. You know the rest."

But I didn't know the rest. Not the truth I had to know. "I mean...why did she leave me?" I could barely say the words.

Lana sighed. "She didn't want to. She wrote us that. The people at the home had someone lined up to adopt. But after you were born, she wanted to keep you. So Aunt Shirley stepped in. She said she'd take you on. There were rumors back home, but..." Lana smiled. "Good old Aunt Shirley. I think she enjoyed the gossip. True fightin' Irish."

It didn't take an Einstein to add up sixteen and ten. "But she's almost twenty-six now. She *could* be my mom now. She shoulda come back when Grandma died. She should...she should – " I thought of Ernie and knew this time I would be sick. I swallowed and swallowed before running to the kitchen sink. I threw up on cigarette butts and soggy pretzels.

Lana had her arm around me and a wet cloth pressed to the back of my neck, and after a while, she walked me back to the sofa and pulled me down beside her.

"I don't know where she is. No one does."

I sat up. "But that woman said...that woman last night. She said she saw her!"

"Joanie knew Rita years ago. She didn't know the

story about her dying. But she says it was Rita. I asked her and she swears it was. Joanie called to her and she turned around. So it must have been her. But then…then she turned and ran. Joanie says she recognized her. Rita recognized Joanie, I mean."

My mind was speeding. "But if she's here? If she's here she'll call you, right? She'll want to talk, right? And you'll tell her about me. And she'll be thrilled to find out I'm okay and I'm by myself, and she'll want to take me, right?"

Lana took my hand. "It was more than a week ago. Why hasn't she called? I think…I think maybe she can't do it. Can't take on – it was a long time ago."

An idea! "Where did Joanie see her? We could go. Go look for her. We could drive around and around and – "

I knew how stupid I sounded.

"Joanie saw her downtown, shopping. Needle in a haystack, Cassie."

No. No. No. I want Rita. I want a mother.

I knew I couldn't stay with Lana forever. I would not go back to Hazel's house. *Rita has to come for me. She has to.*

Somehow we got through the day, and some time during the night, I woke up with the whole thing figured out.

Chapter Sixteen

I went back to school on Monday and watched the time creep by. At 3:45 the bell rang, but I did not take the bus. I went to Hazel's house.

I knew she wouldn't be home. On Monday she played bridge, and I had a couple of hours until Ernie showed up – unless he was drunk and already home. I'd find out soon enough.

I walked around to the backyard and saw the small basement window open – airing out the stinky couch. I wiggled around and pushed and shoved, and in a minute, I plopped down to the couch. I jumped off as if it was on fire. On a hunch, I ran my mittened fingers under the cushions and came up with a handful of coins. Into my pocket.

This isn't stealing.

Upstairs and into their bedroom. Looked through every drawer and under the mattress and in the closet. I found lots more coins and even some one- and two-dollar bills in Ernie's pockets and took them all.

But I didn't find what I came for. It had to be here. Because, wouldn't Rita write to Lana? She wouldn't know Lana was married. Rita would send letters here, asking for information about me. I knew this for a fact. Like the sun rising is a fact.

I pulled everything apart and dumped it all on the floor. I wasn't trying to be neat. Let them think they'd been robbed.

I went by the bathroom and stopped. Checked out the cupboard and found the enema box and carried it into the kitchen. There was a pot of stew on the stove and I lifted the lid and put the ball and hose on top of the meat.

I went through the kitchen cupboards. Nothing. I dropped the cutlery drawer on the floor and watched with great pleasure as the forks and spoons and knives slid and bounced on the gray linoleum.

He had his belt all the way out of the loops and thrashed it down on the counter before I saw him. The table was between us and he shoved it into my stomach, pinning me against the wall. I'd never seen such mean eyes, but he was smiling.

Somehow I slipped down to the floor. I grabbed a fork and stabbed it into his leg. He howled, and I scrambled out from under the table and was on my feet running to the front door. I swiped my arm at a vase and sent it smashing to the ground. I heard him slip on the water and stumble, and knew he was down on all fours, his hand reaching out to grab my foot. I made it to the entrance and slammed the screen door on his face.

He didn't come after me. He couldn't. Not until he put his belt back in to hold up his pants.

Down the driveway. Up the street. Around the corner. A bus was coming and I ran and waved at the driver. He stopped, and I hopped on, not daring to look back.

I didn't know what bus I was on. I sat in a seat and rode until we came to the end of the line. I got off and crossed the street and rode another bus until I had to get off that one, too. I did that for hours, my face pressed to the window because...because what if I saw a woman with red hair?

I got home close to midnight. Lana and Dick were both there. For a moment they looked relieved. Then the shouting started. When they finally shut up I explained.

It turns out I was wrong. The next day Lana said she questioned her mom up, down, and sideways, but no, Rita hadn't mailed letters to Lana at her parents' house.

So.

Nobody wanted me. Lana and Dick didn't want me living with them but didn't know what to do, and Hazel and Ernie wanted to send me to a home for wayward girls. "Like Shirley should have done with Rita," Hazel spat out.

I stayed with Lana until after Christmas. I kept hoping, the way stupid kids do, that I'd get the gift of my dreams on Christmas morning. Rita would be there, smiling, holding out her arms to me. That would be my present. The best present ever.

But...Rita was a no-show.

So.

Off I went to live with some people called Bob and Sue. Cousins. Or something.

I didn't care.

Chapter Seventeen

I went to a new school starting the middle of January and decided to steal a few things straight off. I beat up a couple of kids, too. "Begin as you mean to go on," Grandma used to say. Pretty sure she didn't mean this though.

Bob and Sue decided they'd made a mistake. They really weren't prepared, they said. They bought me some new clothes. And they said they were sorry.

Finished off fourth grade living with Doug and Martha. Kinda liked them, so I held off stealing and fighting (but found out I was a genius at cheating on tests and faking projects). They promised to take me with them to a cottage in the summer. It belongs in the family, somehow, and everyone shares time up there. I've seen photographs, and was really keen about going. So of course, they changed their minds about taking me. Someone came to babysit. *Babysit!* I was almost eleven! So I acted like a baby, pretended I couldn't talk.

I hated fifth grade and hated the teacher and skipped school and stole money from the teacher's desk when I did show up. And so when Doug and Martha went on a holiday, I spent three weeks with Edna. Started school there, but Edna, a widow, said it was too much for her. I don't know why. She wanted me to clean her floors and paint the kitchen ceiling and lug boxes from the attic. I slept in the guest room, but I was clearly a slave. Instead of going back to Doug and Martha's, I went to a new place. Who knows the reason.

Margaret and Frank. They were nice, and they went to church every Sunday. And when Christmas rolled around, I was determined to get a part in the Sunday school play. Most of the girls wanted to be Mary, to wear the blue dress and hold the baby in their arms. But Mary doesn't have any lines. And the whole mothers and babies thing wasn't *my* thing. For me, it was the angel part or nothing.

One Sunday we stayed after church to start work on the play. Caroline Smithers wanted to be the angel. "You won't get it, you know," she hissed at me. "You're new here. Do you know who I am?"

How I hated her smugness. But I stood in front of a mirror and practiced imitating her. "Do you know who I am?" I sneered at myself.

We lined up in the choir loft (the closest the angel could get to being a heavenly presence, I guess) and took our turns. Three girls went, mumbling, before Caroline Smithers got her chance. "Behold, I bring thee great – "

"Speak up, Caroline, dear," said the Sunday school teacher.

"Behold, I bing tee…."

All the girls giggled.

"Start over!"

"Fear not!" I hissed at her.

She shot me a dirty look, too stupid to know I was trying to help.

"Behold. Um. Behold. Great tides…um…of…" Caroline trailed off, forgetting the words.

Oh, for Pete's sake. I jumped up and bellowed: "Fear not! I bring thee good tidings of great joy." I spread my arms wide (for wings). "For unto thee this day is born a child."

I didn't get to finish because several people were clapping.

Instead of the old moth-eaten costume in the church storage, Margaret made me a brand-new one. It was shiny white satin and sheer chiffon with silver lace angel wings.

It was so beautiful. I cried when Margaret gave it to me. She made me a halo out of tinsel and a clothes hanger and pinned it into my hair. I remembered my beehive with Liz and when I was alone I teased all of my red hair out around my head and left it like that.

On Christmas Eve the others in the play paraded slowly up the aisle to the altar-turned-manger and took their seats in the straw. I stood in the loft and suddenly knew I was going to cry. Candlelight and organ music and people singing in the dark. I almost missed my cue, I was so choked up. Everyone knew I was supposed to start, and so everyone turned to look up at me, wondering if I had stage fright.

A thrill charged through my body. I felt electric. I spread my arms and spoke in a voice that didn't seem to be mine. I didn't miss a word. When I finished, I wanted to do it all again. And again and again and never stop.

There was silence. The choir was supposed to start up, but the master paused for a moment. Everyone was staring up. I lowered my arms, and the hymn began.

Afterwards, Margaret told me I was stunning. Stunning! She said, "You looked a vision up there."

Her kindness made me cry.

In January, probably thrilled with the success of having me attend church, Margaret and Frank thought I should do something called Girl Guides.

Every Monday night a bunch of girls got together to sew and knit and light matches, and earn badges and sing songs around a fake campfire in a church basement and say things like twit-twit to-woo. I was the only one who could light matches.

I lit a fire in the church bathroom and the fire trucks came. I promised not to do it again. I didn't. But I did get caught shoplifting.

Margaret and Frank were sorry. I could tell. But they said they thought I was out of control and too hard for them. I promised, and I saw them look at each other. And I knew. And for the first time, I was mad at myself. I could have stayed there. They were nice. I should have done better. Tried harder.

It was my own fault.

Off to Cathy and Philip by the end of the month. Distant cousins, I think. She had great clothes and was so pretty, and I drooled over her John Lennon hat.

I liked them. They were a little older than Lana and Liz. Cathy had known Rita and promised to tell me about her if I behaved.

"Do we have a deal?" she asked.

Why on earth I should behave just to hear about my stupid loser mother was beyond me. But I didn't want to move again. I didn't want to blow it again like at Frank and Margaret's.

So I behaved.

Cathy had hung around with Rita in elementary school. "She was funny and smart and had so many friends."

"Yup. That's why she got pregnant – funny and smart and..." I suddenly remembered Mrs. Huggins. "And a little too friendly with the boys," I added in a snotty voice.

"Maybe you're too young to understand."

"Understand what? Why she doesn't want me?"

Cathy sighed. "One day...well, one day, I hope you'll forgive her. She didn't have an easy life."

"Yeah. Real tough being the youngest-ever prom princess at her school."

"That's not what I meant. When her dad took off, the kids teased her a lot. She made up for it by being brighter and more dazzling than anyone else. I think after a while, everything just kind of caught up to her."

"What do you mean, 'her dad took off?' What do you mean?" No one had told me this. *Anton Jovanovich took off on Grandma?*

Cathy looked guilty. But she took a deep breath. "Sorry. I thought you knew. Rita's dad – your grandfather – embezzled. He was an accountant. It was so embarrassing for Rita, going to school, knowing everyone was talking behind her back. Anton was supposed to go to jail, but the company decided not to go after him. He got a job pumping gas. One day, he was gone. I remember my mom saying Shirley aged a dozen years overnight. Rita was in eighth grade. In high school she tried to leave the past behind."

And so...and so she set out to be the best. I realized something at that moment. I wasn't at all like my mother. Rita gets bad news and shines. I get bad news and become a thief, a cheat, a liar, a pyromaniac.

Shame and trouble. That's me, folks.

Some of the fight left me. Maybe I understood Rita a bit, after all.

So I behaved myself and helped out a lot and studied hard and things sure seemed to be improving. One night Cathy and Philip even said they wouldn't mind me living with them permanently. They couldn't have kids of their own. When I asked why not, Cathy got me a book and sat down and explained what she called the birds and the bees. She wasn't squeamish about it. Just told me straight out all about women's bodies and what happens to us and how we get babies.

I liked when she said "us."

The part about getting babies was stupid and I tried to imagine how Rita could do such a thing at fifteen. I was eleven and there was no way. No. Way.

And she told me it didn't look like she and Philip could ever conceive a child and maybe I'd like to live with them as their adopted daughter.

I remember something hard and tight letting go in my chest. I remember hearing birds and feeling as if my heart might fly up to the treetops with them. I hummed the Beatles – "She Loves You" and "I Want to Hold Your Hand" – and I played with the other girls in their skipping games and didn't trip anybody once. I remember thinking I could forgive Rita. I remember feeling astonished when I saw a crocus pushing through cement, determined to bloom.

One day I raced home from school with huge news. "Guess what?!" I yelled. "You'll never guess!" I couldn't wait. "I got a part in the school play," I said. "The evil stepmother in *Cinderella*."

"Why, that's wonderful, Cass."

But at the end of May, Cathy said, "I have some good news, too. I'm going to have a baby!" She had her hand on her tummy and she was humming.

And then…

"So you do understand, sweetie?" she said. "We'll need your room for a nursery."

Dizzy. Drowning. "But I can help. Honest. I'll take care of you and do work around the house. I can do all sorts of things. Cook and clean – anything. Just name it. You won't be sorry."

"I know. I know I wouldn't be sorry. You are a really good kid, Cassie. I really mean that. It's just…I really can't manage both you and a new baby. But don't worry. We'll find a really good place for you. I promise." She wouldn't look at me. And I really didn't want her to say *really* one more time.

Cathy was throwing up a lot and Philip said to stop pestering her.

She didn't make it to the play. Everyone said I was the most evil, awful stepmother they'd ever seen.

In July, Cathy took me to a store and bought me go-go boots. When we got home, Hazel and Ernie were waiting. Said they were willing to take me back. I screamed. I punched and kicked and bit. Ernie grabbed me and picked me up. I stole Cathy's John Lennon hat from the hook. Out the door. Thrown into the backseat.

I won't write about the next couple of days. I ran away.

Lana found me. She went to the soda shop near High Park and there I was, spending the money I stole.

Next day, she drove me to Doris and Ray Fergus. I thought I'd scream if I met any more relatives!

I ripped up my photo of Rita.

★★★

This time, when Leanna finished reading, she didn't say anything. She didn't look at me. She started sobbing.

"I can't bear it. I can't."

"Leanna..."

"In books, it isn't like this. I mean, it might be, but one knows it isn't real. One knows it's fiction. But you...your life..."

"I told you before I'm glad I'm writing it. Honestly. It's weird, but I feel powerful. I don't know how to explain it." I could see Leanna was searching for one of her words to explain it, so I cut her off. "When I write it, I make it mine. My story belongs to me. I'm...I'm the playwright. I'm the producer. I'm the director. I'm the *star*." I smiled. "They're the characters in *my* play, and they can lump it."

"That's it! You're right! And what would they think if they knew you were writing about them? If they knew what you really thought? Wouldn't they be shocked?" Leanna wiped her eyes. She wasn't crying anymore.

"Children should be seen and not heard," I said with my mouth pursed up like a bitter old frump. Mabel. Hazel. Edna. "And little jugs have big ears."

"There's a child among you taking notes."

"What?"

Leanna shrugged. "It's from a poem. That's all I know."

We smiled at each other. Best friends. Somehow, the two of us went together like peanut butter and grape jelly. But I'm getting ahead of my story. In the story I'm writing, I'm about to meet Leanna.

"I hope you're going to be nice to me," she said when I told her.

Chapter Eighteen

Doris showed me the guest room. Here, at least, I had a big queen bed all to myself. I wanted to lie down and sleep for a week. But first, I wanted to shower for hours in the hottest water I could stand.

"Unpack, and then we'll talk," said Doris.

By talk, she meant she was going to tell me what was what.

"I've put around that you are a second cousin's daughter and your parents are dead. Understand me?"

I nodded. "Don't tell anyone about Rita."

"That's right. It will only make things difficult for you."

She meant difficult for *her*, but I didn't want to make trouble on the first day. Later, maybe.

"There are a lot of girls around here to play with. I do hope you will be nice." She smiled, but there was ice behind that smile.

Again I nodded. Cathy told me Doris and Ray always took a week at the family cottage. I really wanted to go. After all, if it was a "family" cottage, wasn't it part mine? So...I would be good.

The neighborhood girls were waiting after supper. They came to the front door to meet me. Doris put her hands on my shoulders and pushed me outside.

They told me their names and said it'd be great to have someone new to hang out with and then one girl – Kathy – pointed at a kid down on the sidewalk with a buggy.

"That's Lee," she said, and added, "Really lame." She put her finger to her head and did the thing for crazy.

We all heard this huge burp. Lee had a baby on her shoulder and the baby belched and threw up. Lee looked like she was going to pee her pants. She put the baby in the buggy and ran up the street.

All the girls giggled and I recognized them. *Patty Huggins and her stooges all over again. Yank the puppet strings.* They looked different, but they were exactly the same. This time they were after Lee. *Not my problem.*

"Told you," said Kathy. "She lives next door, by the way.

She'll try to make friends, for sure. She's got this thing for orphans."

I swear she leered at me. And then – as always – the questions.

Are you really an orphan? How did they die? How old were you?

I stood up and yawned. "I'm tired. Maybe tomorrow?" I went inside and leaned against the door until they left. I heard them talking about me, making suggestions about my life. I went to my bed and wanted to sleep, but I was wide awake. I stepped back outside and sat on the porch steps and enjoyed feeling really good and sorry for myself.

Stupid, stupid Rita.

Then she was back, the kid from next door, wearing a different shirt, crossing over the driveway to my side.

Lee had stringy brown hair and the ugliest glasses – pointed cat eyes with sparkles. She had on long shorts and a short top and her stomach stuck out between. Her knees were dirty, and she had saddle shoes. Saddle shoes! Who on earth wore saddle shoes anymore?! Those other girls were wearing brassieres. Lee looked like a baby.

"I love your name. Cassandra. Sounds Russian and mysterious."

"No one calls me Cassandra."

"Oh! I understand! I really do! My name is Leanna, but no one calls me that. I just get Lee and I hate it. It's so short. You can't really get your tongue around it."

Weird kid. "Do you want me to call you Leanna?"

"Oh! Would you? It would mean the world to me! And I'll call you Cassandra always. Cross my heart and hope to die."

"O...kay."

"Leanna and Cassandra. They match, don't they? Almost as if we were twins together and these are the names our mother chose." She shivered. "It's so romantic, isn't it? Say! Do you want to pretend we're twins? And... and...I know! We don't know we're twins! Our mother had to give us up at birth and we find each other and...we become the best of friends, but then we find out – "

"I hate my mother. So shut up. I don't want to pretend anything."

Lee – Leanna – looked so hurt that something inside me backed down. "It's a touchy subject for me, okay?"

She nodded. "Sorry. I was being presumptuous. It's because I read so much, my mother says. Say! Do you want to go to the bookmobile with me?"

I had nothing better to do. Plus, she was really impressed with my go-go boots and John Lennon hat.

She talked non-stop the whole way. She told me who

lived where and what she thought of them. Who cares?! I wanted to scream. And yet…

Leanna didn't think she was better than me. I knew the other girls thought they were. Leanna seemed to think being an orphan made me special. Exotic. And all her talking was to share her neighborhood with me. She actually put her arm around me as she guided me along. She wanted me to be a part of this neighborhood.

Like I belonged.

The bookmobile was a library in a truck. On wheels so it could travel around. A lady gave me a form to fill in and wouldn't you know? I couldn't remember my new address. So I took off. Leanna ran after me and got us a Popsicle and gave me half. She was so determined to break the thing straight down the middle. I was surprised. Most people tell me to be grateful for whatever I get.

I wished she'd stop about orphans though. I felt crummy fooling her.

It was still hot but getting dark, and kids were running around the streets playing. Boys and girls together, big and little, yelling and laughing. Someone called, "Come play, Lee. Bring your friend!" Leanna grabbed my hand and we ran across the street to hide behind a car.

Leanna didn't put her fists on her hips and say, "She's not my friend, stupid!"

We squatted behind the wheel and I could smell gas and rubber and banana from the Popsicle, sticky on our hands. Leanna had her finger to her lips. "Shhhh!" Her glasses were smudged and crooked on her nose. She pushed in closer to me, and I could smell baby powder.

You know what? I've never had a friend. There was no one I wanted to phone or visit me. I decided to give Leanna a chance.

Chapter Nineteen

The next day, Leanna wanted to be my best friend. Great – I'm supposed to go from no friends to having a best friend overnight.

"Why?" I asked her.

"Because you're an orphan," she said. Then she said she wanted to be an orphan. I yelled at her and slammed some doors. Doris sent her home and then had a "sit-down" with me.

"Lee's parents are good neighbors, and I won't have you making a scene."

She poured me a glass of Tang. "You are welcome in this house as long as you behave. I knew your grandmother.

I like to think she knows you are here, and I am doing my best for you. But."

Grandma. I gulped my juice to keep from crying. *Why sad?* I'd had almost four years to get used to my life. *Why cry now?*

"Lee would be a good friend for you. She isn't like some of the other girls around here."

No kidding. Leanna is goofy.

Doris looked out the window and said Kathy was coming up the drive. "I don't want you playing with her, Cass. She's too...too mature." She pinched her lips together.

So, of course, I went with Kathy to her house just to bug Doris. Her bedroom was in the basement so she could have privacy from her little brothers and sisters. It was a girly room – pink and silver. Would I ever have a room I could decorate?

Kathy wanted to talk about boys. And kissing. And bras. And her clothes. And her. Just her, over and over.

She did have lots of records. I played some while she changed into all her outfits.

"Well?" She twirled and posed each time, hand on waist, hip jutted. "I want to be a model. What do you think?" She sucked in her cheeks and pouted her lips.

At least she didn't ask me any orphan questions.... She didn't ask anything about me.

"The girls around here are so immature," she said. "I could tell right away you're different."

"How?"

"Well, because you have the right clothes. You'd look okay beside me."

"What about Leanna?"

"Lee? You joking? She's terrible. And she's bossy. She's a real know-it-all." She did a fake shudder. "She wrote a play last year and put it on for the school and she didn't ask me to be in it." She tossed her hair.

Then Kathy wanted to act out this thing where I was a go-go dancer and danced on a table behind her as she pretended to be Dianna Ross – "Stop! In the Name of Love" – watching herself in the mirror. When I hopped down off the table and moved out in front she had a fit.

"What are you doing? *I'm* the star!"

Caroline Smithers all over again.

"I've had drama lessons, you know. I'm going to be an actress, like Patty Duke. Have my own TV show."

She pulled me to the mirror. "Look. Look at us. Look at me. Now...which one of us is pretty?"

Her walls were covered with pictures from magazines. Photos of Petula Clark and whatshername from *Bewitched* and Gidget and Jean Shrimpton and Julie Christie. None of them looked like me.

"My mother was gorgeous," I said.

"Well, you're not."

I shook her off and looked around for my hat. She grabbed my arm. "Don't go. I could help. We could fix your hair and you could use my makeup and…"

She looked so desperate I almost stayed. But she didn't want me for me. She wanted another mirror.

On the way out I saw the beer mugs Leanna had told me about – the ones Kathy's father collected with bare-naked ladies for handles. I imagined someone touching them – a hand on a bare bum – and felt sick.

I went home. I'd been here less than a day, and I'd already ruined two friendships.

I heard a slight cough and there she was – goofy Leanna back again.

"Why do you want to be an orphan?"

She sat down. "Because my favorite books are about orphans! Because you can do what you want to do. No one tells you what to do. It's a very romantic life."

"You're an ass. I don't have one moment of doing what I want to do. Everyone I've ever stayed with tells me *do this, do that, or else.*"

"But that's awful! You're an orphan. People should be extra kind and – "

"Well, they're not. But here's the deal. If you want to

be friends, you have to shut up about orphans. I'm sick to death of being reminded. Okay?"

She looked like a little girl who'd lost her dolly. I sighed. "What do you like doing?"

"Writing! I want to be a writer when I grow up. I've written a play. Wanna see?"

Well, I wanted to be an actress. So I said yes. And besides, I remembered the smugness of Patty and Caroline and now Kathy. I wasn't good enough for them, and they were bestowing a favor – queen to peasant. But Leanna – Leanna's face was open and smiling. Nothing hidden or smug.

I went from giving Leanna a chance to thinking it might be fun.

Chapter Twenty

And so we put on a play. I read Leanna's script, and I liked it. I played the evil witch and did most of the directing. We spent lots of time discussing how to make it work, out there in the backyard under trees.

"What about the curtain?" I asked.

"We could hang a blanket between these two branches. And then the fairies could crawl out from under and greet the audience." She jumped up. "And the fairies could lift each corner and pin it back to these trees. And – Oh! It would be magical!" She whirled around. "What do you think?"

Me? What do *I* think? Wow. A first time for everything! But she didn't let me answer.

"Oh! And what if we use Debbie's dog – Tinkerbell. She's huge! She could be the dragon!" Leanna wasn't in the backyard anymore. She was off somewhere, like in a dream world, seeing things I couldn't. "Well? Well?"

Before I knew it, Leanna and I were scribbling down ideas and walking around the streets, asking kids to be in the play. But definitely not Kathy.

We rehearsed for a couple of weeks in Leanna's backyard. Her mom came out and watched. She had this funny habit of sniffling – like she had a constant runny nose. She made rolled-up peanut butter and banana sandwiches and Kool-Aid for us so we could keep working and nobody had to go home for lunch. Leanna complained about her mom a lot. Sometimes I thought Leanna was a bit of a baby.

"If you want to write, just write! Stop mooning around like an idiot." I told her when she complained again about her mom saying she couldn't be a writer when she grew up. Honestly, she was so annoying.

"It doesn't matter what your mom says you can be when you're older. For all you know, your mom won't even be ali…" I clapped my hand over my mouth. My big mouth.

But she didn't get mad at me. She put her arm around me. "I'm sorry," she whispered. "It must be so hard for you."

Yeah. Hard to remember all the lies.

But whenever I thought I couldn't listen to Leanna

anymore, something would happen and I'd change my mind. One day, I said something to Doris that she didn't like. She said I didn't know how to dust properly and I said, "Who cares?" I mean, they never had any company over. Doris slammed her mop against the floor and yelled. "You're heading down the same road as your mother. Above yourself, thinking you know best. Well, not under my roof!"

I was sent to my room to "think things over." Funny thing – I didn't hate Doris. I hated Rita. Would she ever leave me alone? I felt haunted by her. Why did everyone compare every little thing I did to my mother? Why couldn't I just be me?

Doris and Ray went to visit friends that night and Leanna called me to come out. She took me to her secret spot, her sanctuary, she called it. It was behind some bushes in her backyard. She made me lie down and she pointed to the moon overhead and a couple of stars.

It was damp and mosquitoes were out and I imagined worms crawling under me. I was just about to sing that song "going to the garden to eat worms, chomp, chomp, chomp" because nobody loved me for sure, but then Leanna grabbed my hand.

"I come out here lots. I like to lie on the grass and watch the stars move and think about eternity and infinity. And heaven. And death. And love. Do you wonder what it'd be like to love someone so much you'd die for them? Do you love anyone?" It was like Leanna not to wait for an answer, just to keep blabbing. "Do you have a best friend? A bosom friend? My mother won't let me say the word *bosom* but it just means a friend of the heart. I feel a connection to you. I don't know why. Maybe it is our destiny. Maybe we are fated to be together for all eternity."

Eternity with Leanna. Huh. But then... After never being wanted, maybe I just wasn't used to the idea.

I felt the warmth of her body along the length of mine. I listened to her voice in the dark. I could smell rosemary from somewhere and it smelled like the skin cream Grandma used. And it was like Grandma was there, urging me to accept this friendship offered so openly, no strings attached. I didn't have to be somebody's mirror or backup dancer. I wasn't something dirty. Not con-tay-jus. No cooties. I dug my fingers into the earth to hold onto something stable because my world was shifting. To be liked – just for me. Why? Because. That perfect answer. *Because.*

I felt tears sting. And to keep from telling all my secrets, I complained about Doris. When I did cry, Leanna thought it was about Doris. She rolled on her side and put her arm over me. But for once she didn't say anything.

I got out the photo of Grandma and me. I looked at it for a long time. I put it on the dresser and wondered if Leanna was right, that people who love you watch out for you, even when they are dead. She was talking about Rita – and she was desperately hinting around about my dad – but I was smart enough not to say anything.

There was a tap on my door and I was surprised it was Ray. "Mind if I come in for a sec?"

I liked Ray. I liked the way he dressed in a suit every morning to go to work. I liked how clean his nails were when I watched him eat his grapefruit – every morning, half a grapefruit and a bowl of Red River Cereal. I liked the way he smelled – Old Spice aftershave – and the way his hair was so neatly trimmed. I liked the way he sipped his Scotch every day after work – a "smallsy" he called it – and nibbled at his melba toast and his bit of cheese while barbecuing. I liked that he always asked me how I wanted my steak. A whole steak for a girl who suffered through pink chicken and watery stew and spinach gloop.

He leaned against the wall. "So how are things? Heard you and Doris had a bit of a fricassee earlier?"

I was going to tell him my side of it. But I could see Grandma looking at me and said I was sorry, instead.

"Hmmm. Doris and I don't have children. I'm glad we took you on for a bit. You liven up the place." He smiled.

"But be careful, okay? Help around the house, and keep some of your thoughts to yourself."

I nodded.

"We'll be going up to the lake soon. Wouldn't want you to miss out on that because you and Doris can't get along." It wasn't a threat. More like he was explaining something obvious to a dunce.

The lake! It is *true!*

"So show Doris you're grateful." He moved to the door. "And this is just between you and me." He opened the door, but turned back and pulled out his wallet. "Here," he said, giving me ten dollars. "Girls sometimes need to buy themselves things, I'm told."

The next morning I was up first. I heated the Red River Cereal and sectioned the grapefruit and did the dishes. Doris eyed me like I was an imposter.

Maybe I was. When I studied myself in the mirror, I looked happy.

Chapter Twenty-One

The play was wonderful. Everyone said so. I made Leanna take a bow as the playwright and everyone signed each other's scripts just in case we became famous.

Leanna's mother said she was too busy to watch, even though it was in her own backyard. She told us not to get too big for our britches and not to get swollen heads. Something about "pride goeth before a fall."

"What is she talking about?" I asked.

Leanna shrugged. "I told you. She thinks being a writer is silly. And she's Presbyterian."

But I saw Mrs. Mets watching from behind the bedroom curtain. I wondered if she was just afraid we'd all get our hopes up. And if that was it, well, I understood about not getting your hopes up.

I'm now at the part of my story I don't want to write. I felt like such a hypocrite. (Leanna taught me that word.)

I was asleep and Doris shook me awake. "Where's Lee?" When I didn't answer, she shook me harder. "Cass. Where is Lee?"

"I don't know. Why?" I stared at her head. I'd never seen her in the middle of the night before, so I didn't know she wrapped her hair in a net. She got it done once a week, every Friday afternoon, at the beauty salon. She never washed it or brushed it in between.

Doris sat on the bed. Crumpled down. I saw her chest heave. She took a big gulping breath. "It's her father. Mr. Mets. Marjorie found him." Doris put a hand to her heart. "He's dead. Earl is dead, and we can't find Lee." Her voice rose in a wail and I scrambled from under the sheet.

"I know. I think I know. I'll go." I ran out of the house in my bare feet. All the lights were on next door. I climbed the back fence and slipped across the wet grass to Leanna's sanctuary.

She was curled in a ball, asleep. I didn't want to wake her. Until I did, she didn't have to know. I remembered how I felt when Mrs. Huggins said my grandmother was dead. I did not want Leanna to feel like that.

"Leanna," I whispered. "Leanna. Wake up. You've got to wake up."

She stirred and looked at me and then took in where she was. She laughed. "I'm in big trouble, aren't I?"

I told her. Straight out. Like pulling off a Band-Aid. I watched her freeze. Just go completely still. Then she blinked.

"I'm so sorry. I'm so sorry, Leanna. You've got to come inside. Your mother…"

She got up and took my hand and I led her into her house like she was a two year old. She stopped at the door.

"I'm half an orphan, aren't I? I'm almost like you, aren't I?" I saw a look of horror on her face. "And it's my fault, isn't it? I wanted to be an orphan. I said so and now look. Look what I've done."

She ran to her mother and I stood alone, a despicable creature. Even when she came home with me – to give her mom some time to make arrangements – I couldn't tell her the truth about me. Doris gave me a sign, making a face, and I knew what she meant. *Do not blab about Rita. Do not tell Leanna that you are not "like her."*

I didn't see much of Leanna for the next two days, but I went to the funeral with Doris and Ray. I didn't know Mr. Mets very well. He took Leanna and me to the Dairy Queen one night and wouldn't let me pay, even though I had ten dollars. And he took us to the airport and hummed a tune I knew.

"That was one of my grandma's favorite songs," I said.

Mr. Mets smiled. "Ol' Blue Eyes – Frank Sinatra. 'Come Fly With Me.' Your grandma liked it?"

"Loved it!" And it happened again. Grandma was there with me, lying on the hood of the car, watching planes take off. To Bombay? Acapulco?

Leanna started probing again. But Mr. Mets told Leanna to stop bothering me with questions. And he put his hand on my shoulder when we got back home. "Don't be bitter," he said, in a low voice so Leanna didn't hear. "You'll be fine, just wait and see. Don't be bitter." And the day after I got here he gave me some peonies from his garden – huge blush-red ones. "Just be sure to shake out any ants first," he warned. "If I hear Doris shrieking I'll know what happened!" He chuckled and I grinned. Doris shrieking was hilarious.

Lots of neighbors brought casseroles and pies to the Mets. I made sloppy joe one night and took it over. Leanna thanked me but didn't want to play. Her mom needed her, she said.

Without Leanna to talk to, I hung around with some of the other kids. Debbie and I took her dog for a walk. Tinkerbell – one of the stars of our play. One afternoon we met this boy walking his dog. Debbie waved to him, and he came over, and right away his dog got up on Tinkerbell. His dog was half the size and thought he could do what dogs do to a big girl like Tinkerbell.

"David!" Debbie yelled, red in the face.

David laughed and yanked on the leash. "Down, Lucky." He walked along with us, the two dogs batting at each other, and we ended up at the park beside a school.

"Is this Leanna's school?" I asked. Because it would be my school, too, come September.

"Do you know her? Lee?" David kind of lit up and suddenly I knew he was the David that Leanna said she was going to marry.

"This is Cassandra," Debbie said. "She's new. She moved in beside Lee."

"Leanna's father died. Did you know that?" I asked. "Just a few days ago."

He was scratching his dog's head. "Tell her I'm sorry. Come on, Lucky. Let's go home." He started to walk away, then turned around. "Will she move?"

I shrugged.

"It's just...I don't care or anything...but I've got some of her books." He glared at us and kept walking.

"He likes Lee," Debbie said. "Everybody knows that. David and Lee-ee sittin' in a tree, K-I-S-S-I-N-G!"

"Puppy love if ever I saw it." I laughed out loud at my own wit.

I meant to go tell Leanna about David, but I got back just in time to make supper. Polynesian chicken, which was chunks of chicken with a can of pineapple and soya sauce over white rice. I bought everything myself, but Doris said she wasn't sure about whatever soya sauce was. She put on her reading glasses to look at the fine print on the bottle.

"Imported by Dim Chung Trading Company. Hmmm. Don't think we should be using this." She put the bottle in the sink.

I watched her take mincing little bites of her supper, like it might poison her. I checked to see how Ray liked his food, but he was staring at his wife in the weirdest way. He took a huge bite. "Dee-licious!"

"I saw Leanna's school," I said. "Is that where I'm going?"

Doris and Ray looked at each other. I knew that look.

"What? What is it?" But I knew.

Ray put down his fork. "No sense beating around the bush. I thought you understood you were only with us for the summer. Just until school starts. Didn't Lana explain that to you?"

"No." I couldn't swallow the food in my mouth. I spit it into my napkin.

Doris frowned. "We don't spit at the table, Cass."

"Oh, for God's sake, Doris!" Ray threw off his napkin. "Mary and Peter want you. But they're in California till the end of August. Lana had no business not informing you of the arrangement." I guess he saw the look on my face because he added, "They're good people, Mary and Peter. Probably the best people to help you right now. But we'll be sorry to see you go. Right Doris?" And then, the life raft flung to the drowning victim. Ray said, "Here's an idea. Why don't we invite Lee to the cottage? Would you like that Cass?"

"Ray! Without asking me!" Doris looked like she wanted to smack him. "What about the extra work and food and… and why on earth should we? I mean, someone else's child!"

He gave her a look – like he'd never seen her before and wondered how she got in his house.

I knew this was a guilt bribe. It would have been nice to say no in a withering voice and march out of the room, head held high. To where? So instead, I jumped up and hugged Ray. It wasn't much, but it was more than I'd ever had. A week at a cottage with a friend! And as for the other thing…I pushed it from my mind. I shoved it down, hard. I would pull it out and examine it later.

I threw Doris a bone. "Don't worry, Doris. Leanna and

I'll do all the work and all the cooking and you can have a real holiday!" *Yeah right.* What if Leanna and I used Dim Chung soya sauce again?

I ran outside to find Leanna before Doris could respond. But halfway across the driveway, I stopped. Without thinking, without knowing what I was doing, I had thought of Leanna as my friend.

I was going to the cottage with my *friend.*

Chapter Twenty-Two

Doris gave me a duffel bag for the cottage. I refused to think about packing again in three weeks. "Don't be bitter," Mr. Mets had said. Well, I would be as bitter as I felt like, come the end of the month. But not just now.... I remembered Grandma hugging me and saying she was grateful for small blessings. Okay. I'd be grateful for –

With a shock, it clicked. Grandma meant me. She meant she was grateful for me. I was her small blessing!

But I...

It's weird how you don't understand something an adult says when you're little, but it suddenly makes sense when you're more mature. I wasn't shame and trouble to my grandmother. She wanted me. She kept me rather than give me up. She lost her husband, and she lost her daughter, but she would not lose me. And she stuck up for me, too!

A blessing – definitely something to think about. Or contemplate, as Leanna would say.

I packed my two new bathing suits and my two new shorts sets and my new running shoes. It was so sweet how everyone bought me clothes when they were about to get rid of me.

Leanna had news of her own. Her mom was selling the house.

"I don't know what I'll do, Cassandra. Without my sanctuary and my dad's garden. All the trees and flowers he planted!"

Her mom was looking at an apartment close by. She wouldn't have to change schools and friends. Not like somebody I know. I felt like saying "Boo-hoo," but just in time I remembered her dad and kept my big mouth shut. Grandma would be proud.

Leanna grabbed my hands. "I'm selfish. I'm sorry. What about you? Will you miss it here? Will you be in the depths of despair?"

"I don't know. I like Ray. But Doris? She doesn't want me around. I can tell. She likes having Ray all to herself. It's as if – "

"As if what?"

The idea seemed nuts, even to me. "As if she is jealous of me. Because I'm female."

"But you're only a girl."

"I know but...forget it." Still, I knew I was right. Sometimes I'd see Doris looking at me, like when I brushed out my hair. Maybe she was jealous because her hair was so thin and always hair-sprayed to her head.

"I'm only going to Clarkson," I explained to Leanna. "That's not so far away. We can still see each other. So, no 'depths of despair,' okay?"

All the way north I told Leanna about how grand the cottage was. I laughed when we saw the place! What a dump. And it seemed even dingier than the photos I remembered. Someone had left food out, and we had mice, and Ray swore. Doris yelled at him and that made me laugh. Then Doris yelled at me and said something about how ungrateful I was.

"Oh, but she's not, Mrs. Fergus!" declared Leanna. "She is immensely grateful. As am I."

"You talk too much, Lee Mets," said Doris. "You need to learn what's what."

"Oh, I know, Mrs. Fergus," agreed Leanna in her most angelic voice. "Children should be seen and not heard."

I snickered and then we both laughed and then Doris called us hyenas, which made us laugh even more.

Every day, Ray wore an old pair of overalls and a hat that said *Dodgers*. Doris said it was beneath him, whatever that meant. He had a beer with lunch and his Scotch at supper, and when he poured more than one, Doris glared. (Sometimes I'd practice that glare in the mirror. I'm an actress, after all.)

"I'm on vacation, Doris, and I can't help it if it's a three-Scotch day." I saw him lean in to kiss her but her mouth got all tight, and her body stiffened.

Leanna and I shared a room with a double bed that sagged in the middle. Every night we rolled into each other and sometimes we had a tickle fight. Doris pounded on the wall between our bedrooms. Doris and Ray had twin beds in their room.

"Shouldn't married people sleep in the same bed?" I asked Leanna. "Did your parents?"

She shook her head. "They get to sleep in the same room. But not in the same bed. Don't you watch *Dick Van Dyke*? And *I Love Lucy*?"

I knew Lana and Dick slept in the same bed. So did Cathy and Philip. Maybe after you had kids you slept separate.

One day we found a book under the bed. It had a picture of a half-naked woman on the front. We read some of it before Doris took it away and told us we were disgusting. That night we whispered in the dark and talked about boys. We had a lipstick I stole from Cathy, and we practiced making kisses on our arms and on the mirror.

Neighbors came over and said we could join them in their sauna. I knew something about saunas. I told Doris we had to go because after you sweated like a pig, you jumped in the lake naked. I thought Doris was going to explode.

"I forbid you to talk to those…those people! Why, they're *Norwegian*, for heaven's sake! Who knows what their sort do! It's scandalous! The idea!" And then, wait for it, she turned her venom on me. "Of course, it's what I'd expect from *you*, Cass Jovanovich. And furthermore – "

"They're Swedish, Mrs. Fergus," interrupted Leanna.

Doris stopped in mid-sentence like someone pulled her plug out. Ray laughed so hard he had to wipe his eyes. "Got you there, Doris," he said.

I didn't know why, but it infuriated Doris when Ray did things with us. She seemed to want him all to herself. She liked sitting in the shade and reading and she wanted him to sit beside her – all day if possible – drinking iced tea, playing cribbage. He'd last for a half hour and then come find us, usually with a beer. He showed us how to dive off the big rock. He made s'mores at night and carved us sticks for roasting marshmallows. He told scary stories and took us out fishing one day.

Leanna and I put baby oil on and lay on the dock and I got as red as my hair. By the end of the week I could pull sheets of skin off my body. One night I hurt so bad I couldn't sleep. I lay there, prickly all over, and heard tiny little cries from Leanna. I heard her whisper, "Daddy," but I didn't say anything.

And at night we heard Doris and Ray fight a lot. We heard Doris say, "tramp," and of course she was talking about Rita.

One day I let my hair dry in the sun and it fluffed out huge and curly. Ray reached out his hand to touch.

"It's gorgeous!" he exclaimed. "You should wear it like that every day. Eh, Doris?"

"Certainly not!" she answered. "Cass go tie it in a ponytail right this minute!" I didn't. I just brushed it straight and let it fall over my face.

Doris glared at her husband and then at me. And that night, when I heard her say "tramp" she did not mean my mother. She meant…me.

I didn't sleep, and not just because of the sunburn. Wide awake, hatred taking over my body.

Felt sick in the morning. I couldn't push away the reality I would be moving again. The air was heavy with muggy heat – storm coming, Ray said – and I wanted the storm to hurry up and get here. I wanted to stand outside in the rain and thunder and lightning and be ripped apart. It was my own fault. I had let Leanna become my friend. And I desperately wanted to go to her school and for once have a real school friend to hang out with. I had made all sorts of plans. *Stupid me. Should have known.*

The clouds came and blew over. We saw lightning far off over the hills and we could see torrents of rain slashing down far away. But not here. No escape here. I swear my guts were twisting in agony.

Doris put on another layer of hair spray and a kerchief and announced they were going to visit friends after supper. I couldn't eat. They left, and I couldn't do anything. I couldn't sit still. Leanna finished another novel about another orphan and then hinted around about me again, and finally, finally, the storm broke.

The storm in me.

"Shut up!" I shrieked at her. "Shut up! I am *NOT* an orphan, so shut up! My mother isn't dead, so shut up! She – Rita – is alive. She doesn't want me. She left me with my grandmother. But Grandma died. No one knows who my father is. No one wants me! I'm handed off to one relative and then another and another. Do you hear me you stupid...stupid – I am an accident! I'm an embarrassment. I wasn't meant to be here. I'm not supposed to be alive! I'm illegitimate!" I spat out the old, awful, ugly word.

I saw the look of shock on her face. I hated myself. I hated her. She'd never be my friend now. I ran. Out the back door and over the ridge to the lake. I ran until I saw the diving rock and then I was flying through the air – free – and I thought I might never hit the water. I *hoped* never to hit the water – just stay in the air like a bird.

Then she was there beside me as I plunged, her foot kicking me as she splashed down. She grabbed onto me and we sank, down to the weedy, slimy bottom of the lake. I opened my mouth. Could I gulp enough water?

We broke the surface and I pushed at her, screamed at her. "Get away from me! Get away! Leave me alone!"

But she hung on, hugging me, as if she was saving someone drowning, treading water, banging her knees and feet into mine.

"I don't care! I don't care who you are. I don't care if your mother is alive or dead. I don't care if you're Thumbelina! It's you I like. You. It doesn't matter. None of it matters. Don't you understand? Why didn't you tell me? Why did you let me talk about orphans when you're not one? What must you have thought of me?"

I still tried to break away. Her hands gripped my arm and she pulled and tugged. I slapped at her with my left hand and knocked her glasses. And was suddenly so scared I'd broken them or she'd lose them and – I stopped struggling.

She didn't let go of me until we sat down on the rocks. I thought I'd get up and charge off, but the energy was gone. Just me and Leanna and the big ugly secret.

"I'm sorry I lied to you. Okay? No one lets me tell the truth. Everyone is embarrassed about me. I felt awful when your dad died. I almost told you then. I did. You're the first friend...the first nice girl...."

"I'm sorry, too. I was really dumb. It's because...I talk to you. About important stuff, like our play. You want to act, and I want to write, and maybe we really are kindred spirits. When we did our play, we...we talked about *ideas.*"

I didn't know what to say. So I said, "I have an idea." I took off my clothes and dared Leanna, and we jumped back into the lake, naked, giggling like hyenas. Just because Doris said swimming naked was disgusting. I was so sick of Doris.

"Do you remember what the minister said at my dad's funeral?" Leanna asked. "About ashes to ashes, dust to dust? I think...I think we belong to the Earth. But not just the Earth. The Heavens. We're earth and water *and* stars. We belong to all that. Look up there." She waved her hand and drops of water sprayed out and fell, twinkling in the starlight.

I felt weightless in the water. Lighter than air. I tried to find it again, but the hate in me was gone. I stared at the stars. All those stars. There had to be something else out there. Some other meaning. And there had to be some other meaning for me.

I squeezed her hand. "Thank you," I whispered, so afraid I'd break the spell. We climbed out of the lake and wrapped our clothes about our bodies.

Like newborn babies. Clean. All our lives before us. I could start over. No bitterness allowed.

Two weeks later, once again, driving up a street. Turned around in a car. Watching from the backseat. Leanna waved and waved and waved until the car turned the corner.

Shame. Trouble. Snoop. Liar. Thief. Pyromaniac. Tramp. These were all words. Just words. I didn't have to bring them with me. I could leave them behind.

I opened the window and felt the rush of air blow in and swirl out.

I could stop writing now. Leanna is all caught up. But…I don't know. I kinda like it. Writing.

Chapter Twenty-Three

The ring wasn't on my finger. "I've lost my ring!" I whispered. Around us people shushed.

"What ring?"

"Mary's ring. The one with the dime. She'll kill me!"

Shush! Shush!

"Where did you lose it?"

"Here. Now. I was fiddling with it and it slipped off."

Shut up!

"Wait till the movie's over. I'll help you look."

How stupid! Now I couldn't enjoy the rest of *Beach Blanket Bingo*. And I loved Annette Funicello. I wanted to be Annette Funicello. Or Gidget.

As soon as the lights came up, I was down on my knees,

poking around everyone's garbage. *Pigs.* Leanna waved to an usher.

"She's lost her ring. It's silver. With a dime on it."

The usher yelled to another usher. "Kid's lost her diamond ring!" They helped us look with flashlights.

I didn't tell him it wasn't a diamond. It was an old dime, and someone made it into a ring, and I swiped it off Mary's dresser.

It was Leanna who found it, so the ushers never knew the truth. We washed our hands and left the theater and walked along Weston Road to the Country Style for doughnuts. Then across Lawrence and over the Humber River to Royal York Road and back to Leanna's apartment. My twelfth birthday was the week before, and this whole day was Leanna's gift to me.

"Did you bring more for me to read?" she asked.

"Nope. Don't want you to see that next part."

"Because it's about me! You'd better not say anything mean!"

I put my hand on my heart. "Told the truth. The whole truth. Nothing but the truth."

"Huh!"

"But I do have something else. I wrote a play. Mary and Peter keep telling me to express myself. So I did. Not quite what they meant, but...here."

CHOKE:

A One-Act Play by Cassandra Jovanovich

Characters:

CeeJay (a girl in grade six)

Eva (a girl in grade six)

Peter (CeeJay's guardian; a professor; wears glasses)

Setting:

CeeJay's house: very modern with a sunken living room

Act 1: Scene 1

Living room. CeeJay is watching out window upstage center. She turns and runs offstage left.

Eva: (offstage) Man! It's wet.

CeeJay: (offstage) Yeah, yeah. You brought them? *(Sound of door closing.)*

Eva: (Entering, taking off coat) I said I would. *(Pulls something out of pocket)* Ta-dah!

CeeJay: (Entering behind) Export A? You're kidding me!

Eva: Hey! I gave our money to this guy and that's what he bought. Take it or leave it.

CeeJay: (Takes packet of cigarettes and pulls off wrapping) Here. You got matches?

Eva: Uh…

CeeJay: Never mind. Peter smokes like a chimney. I'll find some. *(Pulls out side table drawer)* Yes! Let's do it.

Eva: Can you light a match?

CeeJay: Are you nuts?

Eva: I can't light matches. I even flunked my Brownie badge.

CeeJay: So how are you going to be a smoker if you can't light up?

Eva: (Shrugging) I'll find someone. There's always someone.

CeeJay: (Sighs. Sound of scraping) It's easy. See? *(Blows it out)* Hand me a smoke.

Eva: (Giggling) A smoke. You sound like a pro.

CeeJay: If we're gonna do this, we have to sound cool. Look cool, too. *(Puts cigarette in mouth and moves to large mirror on wall downstage right)* Here. *(Gives cigarette to Eva, strikes second match and lights both)*

Eva: (Inhales deeply and coughs)

CeeJay: (Inhales and coughs)

Eva: Oh man. It burns!

CeeJay: (Inhales and coughs again) Keep trying. *(Stares at self in mirror while continuing to inhale and cough)* We can't go to a party and smoke if we look stupid.

Eva: Well…we look awful!

CeeJay: Shut up. Just do it. We don't have all day.

(Girls practice inhaling, blowing smoke, tilting head up, down, sideways; coughing persists)

CeeJay: You can't grip it like that. You have to hold it like… like a movie star. Like Bette Davis. *(Demonstrates perfect hold and with hand in air moves across stage to downstage left)*

Eva: Wow. You actually look like a movie star!

CeeJay: (Shrugs and takes a drag) Well, after all… *(Suddenly she puts her hand on her stomach)*

Eva: What is it? What's wrong? *(Dashes over)*

CeeJay: Air…. Outside…. I'm going to… *(Dashes to door. Sounds of vomiting heard offstage)*

Eva: (Hurries offstage; shrieks) You're green!

Peter: (offstage) What's going on here? CeeJay? Go inside this minute!

(Three characters enter)

Peter: (Sees cigarettes) What the...CeeJay? *(Deep breath)* Were you smoking in here?

CeeJay: No! I mean...

Eva: I'd better be go....

Peter: You're not going anywhere. Sit down. Both of you.

(Girls sit on sofa downstage right)

Peter: Well?

Eva: We just wanted to try it because –

CeeJay: (Interrupting) For homework. For a project.

Peter: I wasn't born yesterday, CeeJay.

CeeJay: No, really. For school. About...about the evils of smoking. Why we shouldn't do it. We just wanted –

Eva: First-hand experience.

CeeJay: Yeah.

Peter: Hmmm. Okay. I'll buy it. *(Picks up package, takes out two cigarettes, lights them)* Here. Let's see you. No! Wait! I'll get the camera and take a picture. The teacher will love it! *(Runs offstage)*

Eva: Think he believes us?

CeeJay: Are you an idiot? He teaches at a university!

Peter: (Hurries in with camera) Okay....Now! Inhale. Both of you. Atta girls.

CeeJay: (Inhales and coughs)

Peter: (Snaps picture: flash goes off)

CeeJay: (Hands cigarette to Peter) Okay. What's the deal?

Peter: Deal? Why, whatever do you mean?

CeeJay: Cut it out. You caught us, and you have proof.

Eva: (Hands cigarette to Peter) My mom will kill me.

Peter: Are you ever going to do this again?

CeeJay and Eva: No.

Peter: Yeah, right.

CeeJay: I said no, and I mean it. You want to know why? Because I looked stupid. In the mirror, I mean. *(Brandishes hand at mirror on wall)* There's no point if you don't look cool.

Peter: (Looks at both girls hard) Okay. I believe you. So here's the deal. I won't tell. But I'll keep the photo and if I ever smell smoke on you, you'll be sorry. Oh...and I get to keep the cigs. Not my brand, but what the hell. *(Exit, stage right)*

Eva: Can we trust him?

CeeJay: I think so. He's a smoker. So that means he probably did what we did when he was our age.

Eva: You gonna try it again?

CeeJay: (Shaking head) You mean, go to some party and throw up? Nope. *(Raises fist in air like Scarlett O'Hara)* As God is my witness, I'll never smoke again!

THE END

Goody-goody Leanna was shocked. "For real? You did this for real?"

I tried to look cool. "But of course, *chérie.*"

"But, I mean, didn't you get in trouble? Not just what you put in your play?"

I shrugged. "Peter and Mary both smoke and all their friends do, too. So they weren't really mad. Actually, I know Peter told Mary. I heard them laughing. I just know they were laughing about me." I grinned.

"Are you still happy, Cassandra?"

"Yeah. It's weird. Their lives are so different from anything I ever knew. Sometimes I feel like I'm from another country. I mean they talk politics till I can't stop yawning. The people who come over – so serious. When I tell them I want to be an actress, they look like I'm beneath them. But, Leanna! Some of the boys are so cute. And they wear clothes from Carnaby Street and bring over records I've never heard. I have a crush on one guy, but he's twenty-three! His name is Sebastian and he has really long hair and he wears black all the time. Mary says he's a beatnik. I told him I'm in love with The Monkees – Davy Jones the most – and he said he'd like to help me broaden my mind."

Leanna frowned. "But then, if it's all so great...why'd you take Mary's ring?"

"She says their home is my home....This sweater is hers, too. Do you like it? I can sneak it back before she knows. I made sure to put on lots of deodorant so I wouldn't B.O. it up."

Leanna gave me a funny look.

"What?" I said.

"You said you wouldn't steal anymore. You promised."

I rolled my eyes. "It's not stealing. I'm putting it back. And what's it to you?"

She looked like she might cry. "Because I don't want a friend who steals and smokes and...and.... And because you promised. You vowed. You said you'd start fresh. You said –"

"You are so annoying Leanna Mets!"

"Fine! Then go be best friends with Eva! Go hang around with the cool kids! And beatniks! See if I care!"

"You're just jealous. Admit it."

I thought she was going to yell again, but she sort of

collapsed. "I am. I am jealous. I don't want to lose you. I don't want you smoking with Eva and getting into trouble. I hardly ever see you anymore, Cassandra. And I miss you. Really and truly from the depths of my heart."

Oh, brother.

"Fine. I don't know why I took her stuff. Okay? Feel better? I don't have to do that anymore." I had an idea. "Can I borrow a top? I'll take off Mary's sweater right now."

I pulled it over my head.

"Oh, my goodness!!!! What are you wearing????"

Leanna meant my new pink bra with red rosebuds. "Mary bought it for me. She said a lot of women don't want to wear bras anymore. Something about a show."

"*Chauvinism*," Leanna stuck in. "I'm not exactly certain what it means, but it's something about boys thinking they're better than us."

"Mary talks a lot about men controlling women. She said it was my decision to wear a bra or not." I turned this way and that in the mirror. I could give myself cleavage if I squished myself together!

"I had…something happen this week," Leanna said. "I went after school to Simpson's."

Leanna's mom works downtown in Simpson's Inner Foundations – bras and girdles and underwear.

"My mom was helping two older women – sisters – in

the change room. I was waiting for her to finish because we were going for supper. She asked me to get another size and gave me the box and when I brought it back..." Leanna gulped. "I saw..."

"Them naked?"

She shook her head. "No. They had bras on. I saw their arms. They had these things. Numbers. And I stared. I couldn't help it. And that's when one of them – she saw me staring – and she said 'Auschwitz.' I didn't know what she meant. She could see that and so she said 'The Nazis did this to us. To our family.' And then I knew because I've read Anne Frank. But...oh, Cassandra! To see it! On their arms! I felt sick. It was suddenly so real. Not just in a book. It was awful." Leanna grabbed my arm and pointed. "There. To have a number – not even your name.... Could you imagine it, Cassandra? If it happened to us?"

I hugged her. "Don't. Don't think about it." She squeezed me back tight. Stuff gets to Leanna. "Let's have some tea, okay?" We got out mugs and boiled water. "They talk about war all the time. Peter and Mary. They went to a meeting, a huge meeting, last summer at a university in California. Berkeley. All kinds of famous people were there. Actors and writers, too. They don't believe in it – the war in Vietnam. And they tell me about the protests. And..." I stopped trying to figure it out, what I wanted to say.

"They're so serious, and I know it's important, and I don't want more people tattooed with numbers. But…you're gonna think I'm terrible."

She shook her head.

"Because they're going back to Berkeley again this summer. They say stuff is really happening in San Francisco. They said I could go with them. They said it's their duty to make me aware of what is going on in the world. I care about all that stuff. Of course I do! But…I'll feel like a cheat if I go. Because I just want to see Hollywood. I just want to be an actress. Not all this other stuff."

Leanna put down her mug with a bang. "Don't. Don't you dare feel terrible! Mary and Peter are doing what *they* want to do. They made a choice. Now it's your turn. And if they say express yourself, then they are phoney-baloneys if they only want you to do what they want."

Right. She's right. She has to be right.

"The play's next week. Then we'll see. If I bomb, then… you know that song? 'California Dreaming'? Well, that'll be me. Just dreaming."

Chapter Twenty-Four

The Kids for Kids Theater Company was doing the play in the Eaton Auditorium. It's on the seventh floor over Eaton's College Street. I'd only been on dinky stages in elementary schools. Or in a church. This was a professional stage and I never wanted to leave.

We went over and over all the scenes, stopping and starting for lighting cues. Changing our positions. Getting used to talking and moving on a stage so much bigger than where we practiced. The director sat in the back row and interrupted if she couldn't hear us or if we didn't enunciate. And if we weren't onstage, we sat in the seats and pretended to be the audience. But I loved hanging out backstage and watching the men switch props and change lights and move scenery.

I was the Cowardly Lion in *The Wizard of Oz* – the funny part. When I heard the stagehands laugh, I was on fire. We finished the dress rehearsal and all of us wanted to get something to eat – with our makeup on to show off.

"Absolutely not!" the director yelled. "Nothing says *amateur* like leaving the theater in makeup."

Oh, like we're supposed to know.

We scrubbed at the grease paint with great gobs of cream and ran out into the night. Six of us went to Diana Sweets and we ordered bacon and tomato sandwiches and Orange Crush and pretended this was Broadway.

"We should call ourselves the How-Great-We-Are Club!" said Jean (the Wicked Witch of the West).

And we laughed loud and long because, together, after rehearsal, downtown on Yonge Street, we were IT. Could anyone be happier than us?

Diana Sweets has a box with toy rings they give away at the cash and we each picked a different color and decided they were our good luck charms. No matter how rich and famous we became, we'd never take them off. Friends forever!

We decided to walk up Yonge to the Bloor subway. Heather stopped in front of a door and called us. "Come back! Look! It's a strip club!"

We all ran back and stared at the pictures on the front

– women wearing funny things on their bosoms and teensy tiny underwear.

"Eww," said Jean. "What are those?"

"Tassels and G-strings," said Martha. "That's what strippers wear. You are *so* naïve!"

Martha's in seventh grade and a real know-it-all.

"Tacky," Heather said, pulling her rabbit-fur collar up and doing a stage shiver.

There were eight photos of women and they had names like Velvet and Dee-Dee-Licious and Kitty Cat and…

La Senorita.

The others saw me staring.

"Oh, wow! Red hair, Cassie. A relative?"

Shut up, Martha. Shut up. Shut up.

"Yeah, right," I sneered. "Shut up, Martha."

The door opened, and a man with greasy hair and a scar on his cheek yelled at us to shove off. He lit up a cigarette and said, "Unless you got something to offer? Huh?" He blew smoke in our faces.

We ran.

I didn't tell Mary. I didn't sleep. I didn't eat, either.

Mary was surprised. "I didn't think you'd get stage jitters, Cassie. But a little nervous energy is a good thing before a show."

I let her go on talking, misunderstanding.

The next day, on my way to the theater, I went back. A woman with bright yellow hair was leaning against the door. "What's up kid? Lookin' for a job?"

I shook my head. "I...I have a message for someone. In there."

"Well you can't come in. You're a minor. Give me the message. Who should I give it to?"

"No. It has to be private. The...the man said so."

She shrugged. "Suit yourself. We get dinner break about seven. Between shows. Best bet, go to the back door around the corner."

"Thank you. I'll do that. Thank you."

I ran down Yonge to College Street and took the elevator to the theater.

Into makeup. Hurry! Into costume. Hurry! Hurry! Backstage. Wait for cue. Plan. Think.

Anyone should know what happened.

I blanked. I missed my cue. When they pushed me on, I froze. Could not remember my lines. Nothing. I stared at the other actors as if they were strangers. They stared back at me. I peered out into the black depths of the theater. Nothing.

Finally Dorothy hissed at me and somehow I woke up. Somehow I said something funny about not having any courage.

The director glared at me when I went offstage. "What the hell happened to you?"

"I don't know! I don't know!"

But of course I knew. Rita. *SenoRITA* happened to me. Ruining my life. Again.

After the show, Mary and Peter talked about stage fright and how I shouldn't worry, and I nodded and mumbled and pretended. They wanted to take me out for dinner, but I said I was going with my friends. Back to Diana Sweets. They went to do some work at the campus, and I promised to meet them by eight for the ride home.

I couldn't get rid of Leanna. She saw the others go off without me. She heard them making jokes about me.

"You are not going to Diana Sweets with them so don't pretend."

"Fine. I want to be alone."

"Right. I'm not leaving you alone. You're up to something. I can tell."

I thought about running. Losing her in the steady stream of shoppers. But to tell the truth, I was nervous. "Fine. Tag along if you want."

We crossed Yonge Street and walked a block farther east and into a back alley. It was dark and filled with garbage cans. I swear I saw rats. We almost stepped on a man lying on the cement, an empty bottle by his head. I could smell vomit.

Leanna grabbed my arm. "What are we doing here? You tell me right now. *Right now.* Are you in some kind of trouble?"

"Just shut up, okay?" I whispered. "And leave the talking to me."

I saw the door and a faded sign under a dim light bulb. Burlesque A-Go-Go. I pointed to the photo of La Senorita.

Leanna pushed her glasses up her nose and peered. Then she spun around. "Your mother? You think she's your mother?!"

"I don't know! It could be. Older. But red hair, blue eyes. Pretty. I can't remember. But…" *Why oh, why did I rip up my one and only photo of her?!*

The back door opened and three women came out.

I stepped up to the one with red hair. I opened my mouth. And did my second blank of the day.

"What is it honey?"

I couldn't speak. She pushed past me, shaking her head, hurrying to catch up to the others.

"Wait!" Leanna called. "She's Cassandra Jovanovich. Are you Rita?"

She turned around. "I'm Rita. Yeah. Who wants to know?"

My tongue felt thick in my mouth.

"Are you her mother? Cassandra Jovanovich's mom? Was your mother's name Shirley?"

Bless Leanna.

The woman walked over to us and I could see her clearly under the bit of yellow light.

"Who are you? Who's Shirley?" she demanded.

Not her. It isn't her! Couldn't be! She is way too old. Too many wrinkles. And I can see gray roots. No way she is twenty-eight. Not her. My knees felt like water. I started to giggle.

"Sorry. Sorry." I yanked on Leanna's arm, pulling her as I backed up. "Sorry. I thought you were…" But she had turned away.

I leaned against the building.

Leanna stared at me. "Sure? Are you sure she wasn't your mother? You're not just saying that?"

"No. I swear. But the sign…she's so much younger in that photo. What if it *had* been her? Oh, Leanna – what if my mother turned out to be a stripper?" The relief. The sheer relief made me giddy.

For what would the How-Great-We-Are Club think of me if they found out?

And there it was. The memory of Patty Huggins, telling me I was ill cause my mama was a bad girl.

Chapter Twenty-Five

I slept just great and in the morning, I danced around the crazy sunken living room and sang out loud. I couldn't wait to get back to the theater – to my best performance. I'd show everybody.

"Nowhere to run to, baby, nowhere to hide!" I sang along with The Vandellas.

We had four more shows, and I didn't mess up. Each time I went onstage, I was the Cowardly Lion, just the lion – no baggage or worries in my head to pull me out of character.

And just like when I was the stepmother in *Cinderella* and the angel in church, it felt perfect. I knew who I was. I knew what I wanted. No one could ever take that away. Ever.

Mary saw how happy I was. She said, "When we go to Berkeley in July, we'll see about a side trip to Hollywood. Would you like that?"

I let out a shriek and ran to hug her. And then, feeling like she should know the truth, I told her about Senorita.

"And I thought, I really did, she was my mother. And I was sick. I was so mad at her. That's why I blew my cue. It wasn't stage fright. It was because of *her.*" I remembered Heather. "So tacky," I said, with that same disdainful shiver. "But it's okay. It wasn't her. And I was so happy because how…I mean…yuck. Right? I'd never live it down. I'd rather *never* find Rita than know *that.*"

Mary didn't smile, or nod her head in agreement. She got this look like…like I was her student, and she'd caught me cheating on a test.

"Don't judge, Cass. It's beneath you."

"What?"

"Don't ever judge what a woman has to do, or chooses to do, to survive. You don't know anything about her life or what led her to becoming an exotic dancer. I'm disappointed in you."

Uh-oh. "But –"

"No, Cassandra. No buts. You've been in this house long enough to know how I feel about all the ridiculous double standards and biases against women. You've been part of the discussions when I've had students and colleagues in. I thought you'd learned something. I'm disappointed that you would judge this woman and find fault with her."

Something in me boiled over. "That's not fair! What about me? What about *my* life? I'm female, too, you know. And I've been handed around like a sack of potatoes. I don't know how she – Senorita – got there. But I sure know how I got here!" I could hear my voice getting high and shrill, but I wasn't acting, and I couldn't control myself. "I didn't get a choice, did I? *Did I?* No one asked me. No one cared! No one! Everyone makes fun of me! Everyone finds fault!" I remembered all of the taunts. "Everyone judges *me*! 'You'll end up just like Rita.' So forgive me if I'm glad Senorita isn't my mother!"

I ran to my bedroom and slammed the door. It was *déjà vu*. How often had I done this? Sitting on my bed, sobbing, wanting to die. How dare she? How *dare* she?! But now what would happen? As if I didn't know.

And then she was in my room, her arm around me. "I'm sorry. I didn't think. You're twelve, and I'm a dunce."

It was such a strange thing for Mary to say, I stopped mid-sob and stared at her.

"I…ah…I'm not used to talking to *young* women. So I'm, well, over my head, I guess. But you're right. You've had a challenging life, and *I* have no right to judge *you*." She took my hands. "I wanted you to have some compassion for her, for all women like Senorita, that's all. But I was so righteous that I didn't stop to think. I didn't think to have compassion for a child."

She still hadn't said it. The thing I was dreading.

"We need tea," she said, and I followed her to the kitchen.

She got up on the step stool, and rooted around a top shelf. "How about cocoa instead?" She was holding the yellow tin of Fry's.

Five years old and back in Grandma's kitchen, and if I was to hear the worst – again – then it might as well be over a cup of cocoa.

"So, now you'll send me away? To another relative?" I whispered.

"Oh, honey! Oh, Cassandra! Why would you think – "

"Because. Because I 'disappoint' and then…"

She rubbed her eyes. "Oh, Lordy." She put her arm around me. "Peter and I are not going to send you away. We became your legal guardians. That's forever. Understand? But…there is something."

I sat at the table, wondering. I didn't trust this legal guardian stuff. How much longer till they changed their minds? The end of the school year? The end of the summer? And what about Berkeley?

"You know, I've learned something just now. And it's really uncomfortable. I'm not as smart as I think. I don't know everything. Sometimes being a professor can make one think one knows it all." She smiled at me. "Of course, after all these years you wouldn't want to find Rita at Burlesque A-Go-Go. I dig that. I do. Just...please promise me, Cassie, that whatever you eventually find out, if it's not pleasant, you won't look down your nose at her. Okay? You've heard that saying? 'Don't judge a man until you've walked a mile in his shoes?' Know what it means?"

The devil in me replied. "You mean, don't judge a *woman* until you've walked a mile in *her* shoes."

She laughed out loud and something shifted between us. Really. It was almost as if there had been some energy in the air keeping us apart, but then it floated away like the steam from the kettle.

"Grandma always made cocoa with hot milk, not water."

She unplugged the kettle cord and put a pot with milk on the stove. "Then so will we."

"Is that what you had to tell me? That you aren't so smart?"

"No." She stirred sugar – lots of it – and cocoa together and poured in the hot milk. She was nervous, I could tell. "First, I don't know what happened to Rita. I don't know anyone who does. I know she went to the States for a while, but after? I've always hoped she went back to school. She was very smart. She had every right to go to college or university."

"I just want to know why she didn't come back for me. They said maybe she couldn't. Maybe it was too long and she...didn't know what to say to me? Does that make sense to you?"

Mary shrugged. "Maybe she didn't know how to come into your life again. Maybe she thought you wouldn't want her. But Cassie, Rita was a lovely young woman. She had so many friends. Whatever her reasons, she would never be mean or spiteful or uncaring."

It wasn't much. But it was better than nothing. I took a small sip of cocoa. And with all that sugar, it was...pretty good.

I wouldn't judge. I was sick of being judged myself. I'd be sixteen soon enough. I'd think about it then. Suddenly, I remembered. "You said 'first.' First, like there was a second thing you had to tell me."

Mary opened a drawer and handed me an envelope. Her hand was shaking. I pulled out a photo. Two girls, two boys. One was Rita. The other? I peered closer. "Is this you? With my mother?"

She nodded.

"And the guy with the glasses? Is that...It's Peter!"

"It is. And the other is Ian, Peter's brother. We met in the summer of 1953. The boys were on their way to a camp in Algonquin Park, and Rita and I met them at a party. I ran into Peter again years later at UCLA, and we discovered we liked each other very much."

There was more, I could tell.

My brain worked it out faster than my thoughts and the words just came. "And...did my mother like...Ian?"

"She did. She was crazy about him. They spent a lot of time together that week."

Like Grandma saying she wasn't my mother. There was more to come. "My father. Ian's my father?"

"Yes, Cassandra. And Peter..."

Dot...dot...dot.

"...is my uncle."

Last Page, Leanna!

Leanna is coming with us to Union Station today. Mary and I are taking the train to New York City. We'll spend four days there and see a Broadway show and the United Nations building. Then we will take the train to Chicago. Peter is in Chicago now, doing research. We will rent a car and drive to California. We are taking Route 66. When we get to Los Angeles, I will meet Peter's family – my dad's family. I might meet Ian. He is in Vietnam now, but might be home on leave.

I am packed. I'm not bringing much. Mary says we'll go shopping in New York. But I am bringing Grandma's brush set. Lana brought it over yesterday and she gave me money to spend however I wish. She is having a baby soon and she says it will mean the world to her if I will be "Auntie Cassie."

Leanna slept over last night. At midnight, we snuck outside in our nightgowns and lay on the grass and looked at the stars.

Leanna pointed out Queen Cassiopeia's Throne. "That's you," she said. "Queen *Cassie* – opeia! See how all the stars connect?"

For a moment, I couldn't breathe. Not dots. *Stars*. Connect the *stars* and see what emerges.

I held her hand and whispered, "Make a wish."

My wish has already come true. I am going with Liz to MGM Studios in Hollywood. She works there and said I can take a tour and meet famous actors.

At long last, my road trip to California.

I...am...amazed.

SHARON JENNINGS has written more than sixty books for young people. Her books have received many nominations and awards, including nominations for a Governor General's Award, TD Canadian Children's Literature Award, and Silver Birch Award for *Home Free.* She has taught courses on writing children's books, and has visited schools and libraries both in Canada and abroad to talk to young readers about reading and writing. She recently traveled to Kenya twice as the Canadian juror for the Burt Award for African Literature. Sharon's home is in Toronto, Canada.

A Gutsy Girl Book

The Gutsy Girl Series

Finding Grace

by Becky Citra

"A great summertime read that deals with serious issues in a refreshing manner." —Resource Links

Ages 9-12, ISBN: 978-1-927583-25-8 $9.95
Paperback, 196 pages, 5.25"x7.5"

The Contest

by Caroline Stellings

"With her hyperactive imagination, Rosy is reminiscent of our beloved carrot top." —Quill & Quire

Ages 9-12, ISBN: 978-1-897187-64-7 $8.95
Paperback, 136 pages, 5.25"x7.5"

Home Free

by Sharon Jennings

"This short, sharp story sets the bar high for its followers: it's subtle, wise, and energetic, an honest picture of childhood." —Quill & Quire

Ages 9-12, ISBN: 978-1-897187-55-5 $8.95
Paperback, 160 pages, 5.25"x7.5"